To my parents, Nick and Sylvia Rondinelli.

Forever in my heart.

Lisa Albert

Mercy
Lily

Lisa Albert (signature)

flux™
Woodbury, Minnesota

First Edition
First Printing, 2011

Book design by Steff Sawyer
Cover design by Ellen Lawson
Cover image of girl © iStockphoto.com/Valentin Casarsa
        lily © DigitalVision
Back cover pattern © iStockphoto.com/yewkeo

Flux, an imprint of Llewellyn Worldwide Ltd.

Library of Congress Cataloging-in-Publication Data
Albert, Lisa Rondinelli.
   Mercy Lily / Lisa Albert.—1st ed.
     p. cm.
   Summary: While navigating first love, friendship, and other typical worries faced by high school sophomores, Lily must make an excruciating decision when her mother, who has multiple sclerosis, asks for Lily's help in ending her life.
   ISBN 978-0-7387-2699-1
   [1. Assisted suicide—Fiction. 2. Multiple sclerosis—Fiction. 3. Mothers and daughters—Fiction. 4. Ranch life—Oregon—Fiction. 5. High schools—Fiction. 6. Schools—Fiction. 7. Interpersonal relations—Fiction. 8. Oregon—Fiction.] I. Title.
   PZ7.A3212Me 2011
   [Fic]—dc23

                        2011020383

Flux
Llewellyn Worldwide Ltd.
2143 Wooddale Drive
Woodbury, MN 55125-2989
www.fluxnow.com

Printed in the United States of America

Acknowledgments

While the act of writing is a solitary one, the seed of an idea for a story grows into a full-length novel with the support, nurturing, and encouragement of so many individuals. Without them, *Mercy Lily* would not have had this chance to bloom.

To my family, friends, and readers who offered valuable feedback on pages, chapters, complete drafts, and revisions—I am grateful beyond words. Seriously! Special shout-out to members of my critique groups: Peggy Tromblay, Denice Ryan Martin, Jenny Kloss, Susa Silvermarie, Candie Moonshower, Syrl Kazlo, Sandy McBride, Kathy Witt, Roxyanne Young, Kim Campbell, and Eileen Reiss. Heartfelt thanks to the entire SCBWI tribe, especially the Wisconsin members, whose guidance firmly planted my dreams.

Bouquets of gratitude to the entire staff at the Andrea Brown Literary Agency and my agent, Mary Kole. Fields of thanks to the publishing team at Flux: Acquisitions Editor Brian Farrey, whose vision and editorial advice were invaluable; Production Editor Sandy Sullivan, whose keen eye for detail and continuity blew me away; Publicist Courtney Colton and Publicity Director Steven Pomije, whose combined enthusiasm is infectious; and Cover Designer Ellen Lawson, who created the most beautiful cover I've ever seen.

Undying appreciation to my husband, Joe, for supporting my dreams and believing in me—always and forever. And to my children, Joe and Alexandra, for their patience and understanding and for cheering me on, I am eternally thankful.

One

Parkfield High School's courtyard swarms with students as I walk the mossy path to my bus stop. The two-week countdown until the end of the year has begun, and the anticipation of summer freedom gives the entire school population a chummy energy. Talk of summer parties, graduations, and road trips fill the air. I imagine what it would be like to make my own summer plans.

A group of girls look up from their compact mirrors and nod when I pass. Other students smile or say hello. Some I know by name, others I never will. None of them have any clue that this morning over coffee, Mom asked me to make the hardest decision of my life. She expects an answer soon.

I tune them all out and focus on a cloud in the distance. It changes form. I try to think of nothing. Not school, not Mom, not disease. Nothing.

It doesn't work. Bees buzz in my head as I recall the first time I gave Mom a sting.

—•—

I aimed the misting bottle into the old mayonnaise jar and squirted a few times to subdue the bees. While they settled, I drew marks on Mom's skin, making little X's just like the bee sting therapy booklet showed. My hand didn't want to cooperate with my brain, though.

"How am I supposed to hold on to a tiny honeybee if I can't even hold on to this marker?"

"Just grab it from behind, under the armpits," Mom said, handing me the tweezers. She laughed. "Do bees *have* armpits?"

Her head tremor made her upper body wiggle, but she spoke clearly back then. "You're the only one I trust to do this for me, Lily. You've given the animals vaccinations so many times. I've trained you well as my vet tech, right? Think of it as a shot."

I removed ice packs from her thighs and unscrewed the lid of the bee jar again. The dampness kept them subdued as I dipped the tweezers in. I chased a few around the jar, trying to locate a willing bee. Mom stifled a laugh after I missed snagging a bee on my third try. I didn't laugh along even though I wanted to.

I wanted to give up, call it a day, race to the horse stalls, saddle up Twilight and fly across our golden meadows. But I didn't. I stayed to wrangle a honeybee for Mom.

"Come on, you little sucker." I followed one around in the jar. "Gotcha!" I plucked the bee out of the jar like a prize. Its little hind end jabbed at the air as I held on to its midsection.

Something about this treatment seemed barbaric. Another part seemed to make sense. Bee venom as a holistic healer was totally new to us, and we needed it to work. Desperately.

Mom's face straightened. She motioned to her thighs. "Do it."

A quick touch of the bee's stinger to her flesh made her suck in air through her teeth. The dead bee slumped and dropped from the tweezers. We watched in amazement as the stinger continued to pump venom into her body. It was like watching a nature film in science, only I couldn't close my eyes and look away the way I would have in class. This was real. It was my life. I was certain that no other sixth grader in Oregon—or maybe even the world—was stinging another human being on purpose.

After a few minutes, I scraped the stinger from Mom's skin. Even though I'd read the entire apitherapy booklet the night before, Mom was still giving me step-by-step instructions as we went along.

"Put the ice pack back on and then pour me a glass of water, Lily," she said, swallowing over and over.

She looked pale when I helped her sip, but within a few minutes she was back to her regular self. "Doesn't look like we'll be needing that EpiPen after all," she boasted. "No reaction! I'm not allergic to honeybees! Bumblebees, yes, but not these sweet honey babes." She tapped her fingernail against the glass jar and smiled.

I opened her window blinds, gazed past the puffy clouds to the pure sapphire sky, and wiped my cheeks. "Thank you, God," I whispered.

— • —

The path leading away from school is narrow. Too narrow. I shift the weight of my bookbag to the front of my hip and veer off. I walk wide around a group of goths and their territory beside the chain-link fence. They huddle there, showing off piercings and new tattoos. Shauna Lauri looks me up and down before flashing a quick peace sign my way. I nod in return, then look away when Blake Gunner pulls her into him.

Yesterday she wore purplish-blue bangs. Today her spiky-stiff orange hair could be a weapon. A chunky silver cross hangs from a leather cord around her neck, glistening in the sun. She's worn some type of cross ever since I've known her. It's the one thing that hasn't changed about Shauna.

Ever since grade school, I've witnessed her latch on to one group or another. Sometimes it's hard to believe she's the same girl I made Frisbee mud pies with six years ago. I can almost smell the wet grass, dirt, and pine needles. For a split second, my mind races back to us sitting cross-legged on my porch, a mud pie between us. It seems like forever ago.

I kick a jagged rock out of my way and wish I could've stayed ten forever. Mom was healthy then. Or at least, she seemed to be. Multiple sclerosis hadn't taken over her body. Thoughts of dying hadn't taken over her mind.

I rub my temple in a lame attempt to stop replaying this morning's conversation, but it floods every crevice of my brain. Her staggered words. The anger in mine. I hate arguing. I suck at it. I retreated, and now, making my way across campus, I regret storming out on her.

She grappled for my hand when I hurried past her on my way out the door. "Don't be mad," she pleaded. Then, right before the screen slammed into place, I heard her say, "I love you more than life itself."

"I love you, too, Mom," I whisper, wishing I'd said it to her face earlier. But I didn't love her at that moment. How could I?

A clash of cymbals startles me as I pass uniform-clad band members near the fountain. When the second release bell sounds, I get out of the way. More students explode from the doors and stampede down the cement steps. It's the second Thursday of the month, which means it's Sophomore Social Night. Freshmen get the first Thursday of each month, sophomores the second Thursday, and so on. From what I remember of my one and only time going to Freshman Social Night, it was decent. Fun, actually. They showed a movie in the gym and had pizza. Something to do in our small town.

I'll be missing it tonight. Again. I'm sure some of my classmates think I'm a snob.

I wish I didn't have a good reason not to go. That would be easy. The truth is a bit more complicated.

Mom's waiting for me at home. She'll be at the window, waiting for me to ease her pain. Waiting for me to give her another dose of bee stings. And waiting for my answer.

The sun bakes the back of my head as I pace at the bus stop. I focus on the horizon, where the blacktop meets the sky, and pray for a yellow speck to appear at the top of the hill. *This is pure torture. Why can't the bus pick us up under a tree?*

"Here it comes," someone says, and everyone except me backs up a few paces. Exhaust fumes and a little road dust aren't going to stop *me* from getting in that stuffy bus first. I want out of these sizzling rays.

Jed Abrams rubs his five o'clock shadow and greets me as he has for the ten years that I've been riding his route. "Afternooners, Lily."

The cool cushion hisses when I plop onto it. "Good afternoon, Jed."

I want to curl up and sleep for the half-hour ride home, but I don't. Trent Collins and his buddies are on board today and even though I don't really care why, I still wonder. He's normally either riding with Emily or in his own glossy truck. Maybe his truck broke down or his parents took it away? Maybe little rich boy ran out of gas money? I doubt either of those to be true.

Trent's father, Dr. Collins, treated Mom's multiple sclerosis for years and years before he opened an official MS clinic in Bristol City. Now people come from all over the country for his help. Now he's loaded and spends his money on Trent.

Mom hasn't set foot inside Dr. Collins' office in four years. After we began the bee venom therapy to treat her MS, he told her it was quackery. When she tried to explain about the venom's ingredients and how they work to ease pain and inflammation, he laughed and said BVT wasn't scientific. So she gave him the boot.

I was glad she fired him. All the expensive medicines he had her on seemed to make her even sicker. Blue ones, red ones, capsules, tablets. Nothing helped until the venom, and now I'm a pro at stinging her. Over the past few years, thousands of bees have made the ultimate sacrifice to keep Mom pain-free. Dr. Collins may call it quackery, but we call it holistic.

I rest the side of my head against the chrome bar beside me, close my eyes, and push away memories of Trent by making a mental list for the weekend: *pay bills, clean stalls and cages, bathe Pepper, grocery shop . . .* Then a distant memory of us in Anderson's Grocer creeps in from the corner of my mind. His shaggy bangs covering his eyes as we strolled down the candy aisle and the way my heart leapt when he reached for my hand.

The memory vanishes when I open my eyes and catch him watching me. I flash a courteous smile, turn, and pretend to focus on the road. My mom firing his dad was the beginning of the end of our childhood friendship. There's still this invisible wall between us, and sometimes it's easier to just look away instead of through it.

We're almost to my house when the laughter in the back of the bus turns to a low chant.

"Moon. Moon. Moon."

I flinch when a car honks and then zooms alongside the bus. Betsy is hanging her head out of Emily's little red car. She pretends to gag by sticking her finger down her throat. Emily is laughing and wiping her eyes.

Jed scowls and shakes his head in disgust.

Oh man. Some kid squashes his bare butt against the window while all the other guys howl and cheer him on. All except Trent. He curls his mouth, rolls his green eyes, and scoots away from his gang. *He's not such a bad guy for a pretty boy.*

"It's your stop, Lily," Jed calls, snapping me out of my thoughts. "How's your Mom doing these days?"

The doors fly open and the thick, humid air makes me gasp. I pause. My brain urges me to spit out a smart-ass answer. *She's thinking about quitting, giving up, meeting her maker. And oh, she wants me to let her.* I look him in the eyes. "She's been using her wheelchair a little more and her cane a bit less."

Jed purses his lips and nods. "And how 'bout you? How are *you* doing?"

This question would creep me out and seem a bit personal coming from some other bus driver, but Jed and I go way back, so it doesn't bother me. I've always thought of him as part of the family. Like a second uncle once removed or something, because he was Dad's best friend and over at our place all the time. Still, I can't bring myself to tell him how I'm doing. I don't really know the answer. "Better not let all your cool air out," I say, stepping off the bus. "See you next week."

The bus doors close with a whoosh. Jed tips his hat my way and takes off. In the last window, Trent's watching me. He tilts his head, rakes his fingers through his wavy blond hair, and mouths, "See ya."

I watch Trent get smaller and smaller until a blaring car horn makes me lunge for the curb.

Emily unrolls her window as she slows her car. "Get out of the road. I almost hit you and scratched my bumper."

Betsy laughs her horse-snort. "Nice jeans, hillbilly." Then Emily guns it and spews gravel before driving off.

I shake my fist at the car, hoping she's looking in her rearview mirror. "Witch!" I yell, knowing full well she can't hear me over her blasting music. I let my fist fall to my side and stand there in the dust. It makes no sense to me how one day I was her friend and the next I was nothing. Shunned like a sickly animal in a herd, I was cast away because I cramped her style.

I brush off my overalls and head up the driveway. I smile, because a full day's sun has brought more blooms. Our house looks prettiest in spring. Happy. Yellow, red, and orange tulips frame the flower beds beneath the front windows. The shady area around the porch is covered in little tendrils of ferns unfurling. I take a deep breath in anticipation of their fragrance. If green had a scent, it would smell like ferns.

Pepper comes running from the side yard and I greet her at the hedge of lilacs. Her big butt sways with every wag of her tail. She spins in circles, bumping her butt against my knees before tunneling through my legs.

"Come on, you goof, let me turn on the sprinkler," I say. "Mama forgot about you out here, didn't she?" The second I say "Mama," Pepper hurdles the porch steps and waits at the door. She stares the door down while marching in place.

As I bend to turn on the sprinkler, I catch a glimpse of Mom closing her blinds.

She's in there waiting. Waiting for me to bring the bees. Wanting me to ease her pain.

Water pitter-patters against Mom's bedroom window in an on-again, off-again rhythm. The air conditioner hums and sputters. Droplets trickle down the pane and drip onto the tulip garden below. A plump bumblebee clings to a tulip while the flower trembles in the shower. When the stream from the sprinkler leans away, the bumblebee takes flight.

"Yes, you fly. Fly far, far away from here, stupid bee," I whisper. "You are the lethal kind."

Pepper barks with excitement when I pull the screen door open. She barrels through the kitchen and living room and heads to the back of the house, to Mom's room.

Mom's at her vanity, holding her silver hairbrush. I pause in the doorway and take in the scent of baby powder that fills her room. She smiles into the mirror when she spots my reflection.

"Sit, Lily," she tells me, and pats her bed. Her breathing is slow and her voice shaky. I've become used to waiting patiently between her words. For the past two years, talking has been a struggle for her. And if you ask her, she'll tell you it's too much trouble anymore. So I savor every word she speaks.

"Go on, Mom. What is it?" I stroke her arm and hide my shock at how bony it's become.

"Have you thought about ... my idea?" She blinks hard and swallows before catching her breath. Her hazel eyes twinkle and are full of life in spite of her pain. She smiles and squeezes my hand.

My nostrils twitch and my eyes begin to fill. "You can't give up, Mom." My heart races and I close my eyes, shaking my head steadily. "What has gotten into you? We can call Dr. Collins or find another doctor, a psychiatrist, someone to help you. To help us. I don't want you to leave me." I glance up, tears flowing down my face, to see her smiling.

"I'll never really ... leave you, Lily." She presses our hands against my chest. "You'll always have me here."

I wipe my face and clear my throat. "I don't know if I can do it. I don't know if I could live with myself, knowing I let you die."

"Could you live with yourself ... if you don't?" Her eyes lose their glimmer when she asks me this.

"I don't know!" I slump forward like I was just sucker-punched. I get what she's really trying to say. Which would be worse—letting her go, or watching her suffer? Both will bring me guilt and sadness. Only one will bring her peace.

Pepper nuzzles against Mom. I set her hand on the dog's big head before I go to the window. I open the blinds and stare through the sheet of water. Everything's a blur. *Could I live with myself... if I don't let Mom die?*

A sudden rush of déjà vu comes over me, making my heart ache with memories of Dad. As much as I miss him, it's next to impossible for me to visualize myself without Mom. I close my eyes and try, but she appears out of nowhere, looking peaceful, even happy. First, she's her old self and healthy, then she's suddenly ill and bedridden. I shudder and turn to Mom when she whispers my name.

"Lily." She motions to the window. "Get the bees and ... move the sprinkler."

"Okay," I say. "First, the ice packs." I help her into bed and push her bangs to the side. By the time I go to the freezer and get back to her room, she's dozing. I set an ice pack gently on each thigh and whisper, "Back in a flash."

The screen door slams behind me as Pepper runs ahead toward the hives. She knows the routine. She knows I'm either going to see Twilight in the pasture or to the hives to collect bees. I make a pit stop at the shed and grab my beekeeping veil, gloves, and the bee jar.

Pepper's lapping water from Twilight's trough when I reach the hives. It's hot. Sweltering, pit-stains hot. I pull the mesh veil over my head and neck and yank the gloves up to my elbows. The bees sound hot and bothered, and I don't want to take any chances with pissed-off guard bees. The low hum coming out of the hives gets louder and more intense when I pop off the access plug and hold the mouth of the jar over it. In under a minute, I've got about a dozen and a half lively ones. I only need twelve but it's good to have extra in case any escape or croak. I slip the lid onto the jar and replace the plug.

A bee lands on my veil and crawls in a circle as though it's looking for an opening to get in. I blow and it flies off. Years ago, I would've been freaked out about a bee on my veil, but it doesn't bother me anymore. Our hives were part of this farm before Mom and Dad moved here, and I doubt the original owners ever thought the bees would be used for anything other than honey-making and pollinating. When Mom heard about bee venom therapy for MS, she said it was a sign she should try it since we kept bees. Gone were the days of jars of honey when we began filling them with bees instead.

I whistle for Pepper and she follows me back to the shed. She prances through the sprinkler as I toss my gear inside. She leaps when I yank the hose, moving the sprinkler to Mom's lily garden. Tiger lilies, day lilies, Easter lilies are all beginning to bud atop their stalky stems. Another week or two of spring sunshine will bring blossoms.

A toad burrows into the moistened ground. The earthy aroma of soil and peat moss fills the air and reminds me of the day we planted Mom's garden. Me, Mom, Dad, and Pepper.

Pepper was just a puppy then, six months old and full of mischief. Every time one of us dug a hole, Pepper dug a hole. She ate three bulbs that day and Dad told me they'd grow in her belly and blossom out her butt.

Being seven, I believed him, and gave Pepper a lot to drink to water those bulbs. Mom laughed so hard she cried. Dad said when they sprouted, we'd call them stinky lilies.

I laugh at the memory until I realize it's been two years since Mom has worked in her garden. I know she misses it, too. Her entire collection of lilies began with a single tiger lily—one that I gave her for Mother's Day when I was in kindergarten. After that, hunting for rare varieties became more of an obsession than a hobby. She still buys new lilies, only now I'm the one who gets in there to plant them. She's never said so, but the garden doesn't look as nice ever since I took over.

I turn away from the garden when I hear Twilight whinny from the field. I wave my arms over my head in case he's watching me. He throws his head up and down before galloping away. "I'm itching for a ride, too," I say. I snap my fingers for Pepper and she comes right to my side.

The screen door creaks with a sickening, high-pitched sound. I hold it open for Pepper and nudge her to go in first. The bees are getting angry. I'm getting hot.

Soft jazz plays in the living room where Pepper climbs onto the sunlit sofa. She plops with a sigh, pooped out from her romp in the yard. She's still damp, but I don't mind, so I let her be.

"Summer's on its way," I say when I go back into Mom's room. "Everything's starting to bloom."

She swallows hard. "Move the . . . sprinkler?"

"Yes, I did. And you know what? The smell of the dirt made me think of stinky lilies. Remember that?"

Her face lights up and she nods before letting out a chuckle. "I do!"

"Lots of active bees today," I say, misting them. "It must be the heat." I remove the ice packs from her thighs and tuck them under her neck. I feel a rush in my chest and remind myself to breathe. "You ready?" I watch her face for a blink of approval and grab a bee.

I wince as the stinger jabs into her flesh. I've been stung enough times time to know that it burns. She barely flinches. I know the venom doesn't help like it used to, but her plan to try sixteen stings next time scares me. It could be toxic, deadly. And if it's not enough to help her pain, it'll be her last try ever.

After stinging her thighs, neck, and shoulders, we take a break and she sips some water. I check her breathing and feel her throat for swelling.

"I'm fine," she says. She nods and grins. "Finish."

Six more dead bees later, we're done. She holds an ice pack to her wrist while I dispose of twelve carcasses. I begin to lightly massage around each spot to get the venom moving into her system. I've only rubbed her thighs and neck when Pepper trots into the room, spins a couple times, barks, and then bolts down the hall.

I spread the slats of the window blind and peer outside. I hear a rumble in the driveway.

"Who's here?" Mom asks when we hear a honk of a horn.

I crane my neck to see around the pine trees. "There's only one person in this town who'd come here in a school bus."

"Jed," Mom says. She smiles and winks at me. "Go see ... what he wants."

The doorbell rings three times before I push the screen open. Jed is wringing wet and pale.

Two

The calf is having another seizure." He grabs my arm and ushers me toward the bus.

The last thing I want to do right now is play vet. But Jed's one of our best customers as well as being like family, so I stoically follow him up the bus steps. I peer over his shoulder as he kneels down in the aisle.

His three-week-old calf is lying on her side on the floor. Her eyes are rolled into her head. I feel her tense body twitch and jerk while I check her breathing. "Have you been giving her the medicine?"

"Yes, yes. Why isn't it working?" Jed strokes the calf's head.

"It is working. She's breathing. Open these windows while I get her a booster shot."

Pepper follows me out of the bus and sticks close to my side. She doesn't like going into Mom's clinic any more than any other animal does. "It's all good, Pep," I say. "More animals come out of here feeling better than not at all." She plants her butt on the welcome mat and lowers her ears. "Fine then. You stay."

As soon as I walk into the clinic, I bolt for the employee door, which leads to our kitchen. I open it just enough to fit my head in and yell into the house, "Mom? Jed's calf is having a seizure. Should I give her a booster?" I wait for an answer.

"Diazepam," Mom calls.

I prepare the booster and tap the air bubbles out of the syringe on my way back to the bus. Pepper stays at my side until I get on board.

"She's not as tense now," Jed says.

I smile at him. "Neither are you."

I grab a fold on the back of the calf's neck and slowly inject the medicine. "This is a stronger anticonvulsant. She'll come out of this quickly now."

"It's got to be damn near ninety today." Jed wipes his face on his shirt. "Poor thing can't handle this heat. I hear all of Oregon is breaking heat records today."

"Breaking records?" I blink hard. A vision of Mom with a jar of sixteen bees flashes and fades. A lump forms in my throat. "I have to check on Mom. Come in for a drink."

He pats the calf on the rear and gets up with a groan. "Just for a drink. I have to get her home before nightfall."

I look to the sky as we walk across the driveway. "There's a couple of hours before sunset. You can stay for supper."

Jed smiles. "Another time soon. I've got to get the calf to her mom for her supper."

We're quiet for a minute until I say, "If she has another seizure, call me and I'll come right over."

"I know what you're thinking, Lily." He chuckles and shakes his head. "That I'm a crazy old coot for bringing that calf up here in my school bus. Granted, sixty may be old to you, but I can tell you I am not crazy." He rubs the back of his neck and lets out a long breath. "When I pulled into my driveway this afternoon and spotted that poor thing laying near the fence and shaking, I didn't give it any thought. Just picked her up, put her in the bus, and drove here." He holds the screen door open for Pepper and then me.

The cool kitchen floor is soothing to my bare feet. "Mom?" I call and pour three glasses of iced tea.

Pepper sprawls on the tile. Her hind legs stretch behind her, exposing her entire underside to the coolness of the floor.

"Look out, Frog Legs," I say stepping over her. "I'll be right back, Jed. Mom could probably use some tea, too."

He gulps his whole glass down and smacks his lips. "Ahhh. You go on and say hello to your mom for me."

I turn the corner and nearly spill the drink on her. "What are you doing up?" I grab her elbow and lead her to the table.

She yanks her bathrobe belt tighter, hooks her cane onto the table, and sits. "I want to visit with Jed." She takes a sip of tea and smiles. "How are you?"

Jed blushes and cracks a knuckle. "Fine, Sophia, fine." Another knuckle crack. "It's the new calf. She had another spell."

I pat Mom's shoulder. "I gave her the Diazepam like you said. I think she needs a higher dose." The last two words become stuck in my throat, but Mom doesn't seem to notice the fear they cause me. I swallow them.

She wrinkles her brow. "The calf's in the bus?"

Jed reaches out and holds Mom's hand for a second. "I better get her home."

"Wait," Mom says. She laughs. "You brought her … in your bus?" She motions to my feet. "Get your shoes. Go with him. Take a harness."

My heart sinks. I just want to stay home and keep an eye on her. "But what about your supper?" I say.

"It can wait." She gives me her *I'm serious* expression—chin down, wide eyes—and nods at me. "Okay?"

Jed's gaze ping-pongs between us. "The bus was a bad idea. Next time I'll bring her in a crate or call you to come to me."

"Fine." It's not worth arguing about it, so I do what she asks, especially since it has to do with our vet business and Jed. I hate the thought of leaving her alone when she needs me. Then again, I stay home even when she doesn't. It's not like I ever have any plans. I think my last night out was that one Freshman Social Night. A party animal, I'm not. I slip on my sandals. "Let's go."

Jed gathers the empty glasses and puts them in the sink. "I'll bring Lily back home after I settle the baby in."

"That baby needs a name … soon." Mom smiles and points her cane toward me. "Give him more pills. Add a half dose." She takes a deep breath. "And rub chamomile oil on his snout and neck to help him relax."

"See ya in a bit." I kiss her on the hollow of her cheek. "I'll make you some supper then."

Pepper lifts her head and thumps her tail when Jed cracks the screen door. Mom snaps her fingers and Pepper goes to her side. "I'll feed Pepper." She stands in the doorway and shakes her head. "A cow in a bus," she says, laughing.

I watch for the porch light to flick on as we drive off. Even when it's not dark, that porch light goes on whenever I leave the house. Ever since I was a little girl, like magic, it's always lit up our slice of the countryside.

"Mom," I whisper. Her voice chimes into my memory of younger days. *Lily … come in when the porch lights turn on.*

I slip the harness around the calf and hold on. She's drowsy but standing now, and I don't want her to get hurt on the bumpy ride home. I help her keep her balance. I picture Mom, drowsy and standing with her cane. Balanced. Hurting.

The bus lurches forward. I wrap my arms around the calf's fuzzy brown neck to keep her still.

Jed clears his throat. "Your troubles are safe with me, Lily."

Three

Our eyes meet in his rearview mirror. I want to look away but I don't. *Be strong. Don't cave.* I squint and tilt my head. "Troubles?"

As soon as he looks away to watch the road, I let myself blink again.

"When are you going to name this calf?" I ask.

"I see the way you keep to yourself. On the bus and other times, too." He locks eyes with me again.

I plunge my fingers into the wavy hair on the calf's head and fluff it to a point. "Call her Toughie. She's a strong little thing."

"It's not good to be alone so much, Lily."

The bus fishtails a little as we take the turn into his driveway. The calf lets out a bellow and leans into the turn.

Jed cuts the engine and cranks the door lever, letting in the stink of manure. He lifts his leg across the aisle, blocking my way with his boot. He nods toward the barn and grumbles. "Mrs. Abrams was the one who named all the newborns." He lowers his foot and stands slowly. "I got a handful of animals in there that don't got names."

I scan the barnyard and realize I haven't been here since his wife Gail died two years ago. Her departure to the great beyond was totally unexpected. She'd reclined for a midmorning rest on a typical Sunday and just never woke up. The newspaper was on her lap, and the tea beside her was still warm when Jed found her. "A simple exit for a classy lady," Jed said at her funeral. He was right.

After the service, Mom told me that Jed was lucky. How his wife passing away so quietly was less agonizing than what we'd been through with Dad. I remember how angry that made me. *Lucky?* It was a stupid thing for her to say. I bet Jed didn't feel lucky. His heart was just as broken as hers was.

Looking toward the wheat field, I envision Mrs. Abrams in a flowery sundress, pumping water at the well. The vision fades and I turn to Jed. "She'd want you to name those animals, ya know."

He smoothes his graying eyebrows and lets his fingers rest at his temples. "I know she'd like that, but I just can't bring myself to." His arms fall to his sides and he takes a deep breath.

I give the three-week-old calf a pat on the head and lead her down the stairwell. "Come on, Toughie. Let's go name some animals."

Jed lets out a laugh. "Toughie she is."

We settle the newly named calf in with her mom, Willow, before following the dirt road to the weather-worn barn. I roll the doors open. The pungent odor of urine, spoiled milk, wet hay, and crap makes my eyes water.

Jed pulls out a hanky and blows his nose. "This heat wave sure makes it hard to keep this place fresh."

Crevices in the wood walls let in streamers of sunlight that strobe as we walk through them. They flicker-flash as I slice them by waving my arms. A piglet squeals and Jed laughs.

"Two new pigs," he says, picking them up, one at a time. He holds out the littlest one.

Its skin is warm as a fresh-baked dinner roll. "They're adorable!" The little oinker snorts and squirms in my grip. I rub its soft, pink belly until it relaxes. I take a peek of its underside. "It's a girl! We'll name her ... Sunbeam."

Jed trades piglets with me. The bigger one shivers as I look it over. "It's okay," I whisper, looking into its eyes. "This chubby boy has a sweet face." I nuzzle his flat snout and hear a faint pitter-patter. My foot becomes warm.

Jed laughs and slaps his hip.

I set the piglet down and shake my foot. "Pisser. How's that for his name?"

"Mrs. A would approve," Jed says. He looks to the wood ceiling and grins. "I can almost hear her chuckling."

I follow his stare. "Me too."

"Damn it!" Jed thrusts a fist in the air and jerks his head. "*This* is why I said it's not good to be alone so much, Lily."

His outburst startles me and I jump back. Little Pisser scampers away. "What do you mean? Isn't it normal to miss your wife?" I ask.

Jed turns and leaves the barn. I walk behind him to the dirt road. He stops near the corral and pulls up an old whiskey barrel, then pushes my shoulders down until I sit.

"Yes, it's normal, but I regret a lot of things," he says. "Sometimes I dwell on her. That's why I stay busy, keep driving that bus. Need to get out of the house and see people. I can't bother you and your mom all the time, right?"

My heart skips a beat and I bolt up. "You're not a bother." I lean toward him and smile. "You could spend more time at our place. Maybe help around the farm and clinic? We could use the help, and we'd give you free vet care and meals."

He rubs his palms together and lifts his bushy eyebrows. "Hmmm. That just might be a good plan for all of us. You'll have more time with kids your own age. I'll be less lonely." He wipes his forehead and smiles. "And your mom can get the rest she needs."

I let out my breath and tuck my hair behind my ears. "Right. Mom." I can't bring myself to tell him that maybe, just maybe with him around to help, Mom will be stronger and happier. "One thing, though, Jed. I think this needs to be *your* idea. You tell Mom. I don't want her thinking I can't handle taking care of her and the clinic."

"Along with school and Twilight," he says. He holds up his hand for me to high-five. "Gotcha. I was a tractor salesman at one time in my life. Darn good one, too! I'll talk to her."

"Sounds good!" I rub my sandals in the dirt and notice how long my shadow is. Night is closing in. "I better get home to make supper."

"Sure thing. Hop in my truck." Jed digs in his pants pocket. He tosses his keys at me. "You drive."

Like a baseball player going for a fly ball, I dive for them. "All right!"

The truck shimmies down the gravel driveway, leaving plumes of dust in its path. Jed clicks off the radio.

"Got any plans for summer?" He sits back and rests his elbow on the window frame.

I turn onto Half Mile Road. "Same old routine, I guess."

"But it won't be, with me around." His head bobbles a little and he smiles real wide.

"True," I say. I picture Jed sweeping hair, cleaning instruments, stocking meds, all while I'm out riding. "I'll get to spend more time with Twilight."

I signal for the turn into my drive and check the rearview mirror. A glossy black truck is coming up on me fast. It starts to pass me on the left and honks as it slows down.

"Hi Jed!" Trent yells, and waves. At first he looks surprised to see me in the driver's seat, then smiles wide. "Hey, Lily!"

I'm a bit shocked by his enthusiasm at seeing me. My heart speeds up when I say "Hi" back, but I'm not sure if it's because Trent's eyes are sparkling or because Emily's in the passenger seat, staring straight ahead. Her arms are folded tightly across her chest. I wait for her to shoot me a dirty look but it doesn't come. *Fine, don't look at me.*

"Hi, kids," Jed yells, nodding.

I smile, focus back on the road, and wave before pulling into our driveway. Mom's in the porch swing with Pepper. The porch light above them glows against the cedar siding.

I slam my door and Pepper starts barking her stranger-is-here bark. The hair on her back raises up and she jumps off the swing.

"It's just me, silly," I tell her.

Jed crouches down and claps. "Come here, girl." Pepper almost bowls him over.

Mom stands slowly and walks to the railing. "Calf okay?"

Jed launches a stick for Pepper. "Toughie is fine."

"I named her Toughie, Mom." I toss Jed his keys as we walk up the porch.

"And she named my new pigs, too," Jed says. "Sunbeam and Pisser."

Mom scrunches her face. "Pisser?"

"Well, he peed on my foot."

Mom rolls her eyes. "That's just . . . lovely, Lily."

We're all quiet for a few seconds, and then Mom starts laughing. Jed and I crack up with her.

Our laughter echoes through the valley and a faint neigh joins in. I look to the pasture and spot Twilight, running and kicking.

I rub the back of my neck. "I'll make supper."

"You must be . . . starved," Mom says to Jed. "Join us?"

Jed holds the door and helps her up the stoop. "How 'bout tomorrow? We can sit and talk then, too." He accentuates the word *talk*, and smiles.

"I'd like that," Mom says, gripping Jed's arm as she steps up. She's got her brave face on, but by the way she's shuffling her feet, I can tell that every step is painful. Watching her makes me wince. The venom should be working by now.

"Thank you, Jed," I say as he helps her into the house. I stay behind and whistle for Pepper. She returns with a rock the size of an apple, sets it at my feet, and whimpers.

"Oh, all right. Bring the rock."

Pepper steadies the rock in her jaw and prances inside. She drops it with a thud into her bed.

Mom flinches and turns. "Another boulder?"

"I think that dog is trying to build something," Jed says.

Mom smiles. "A calf in...a bus. A pig named...Pisser. A rock-lovin'...mutt." She shakes her head. "Weirdos."

"Don't forget a horse who kisses," I add.

"Ah, yes," she says. "Go ride."

"I'm too hot and tired. I'll put Twilight to bed after we eat," I say. "Chef salad, okay?"

Mom nods. Jed gives us both a good-bye hug and lets himself out.

After dinner, I put Twilight in his stall and then help Mom into bed. I slip into my sheets as the sky turns orange and purple. A cardinal sings one last song. It's my lullaby.

— • —

The next day at school, I struggle to concentrate. Mom didn't seem any better this morning, and I want to be home with her. The day drags on until I finally get back on the afternoon bus. I'm glad to see Jed, since we had a substitute driver this morning.

"Afternooners, Lily."

"How's Toughie?" I toss my backpack onto the seat behind him and scan the bus. No Trent today.

"I stayed home to check on her this morning, and by noontime, she was alert and hungry."

"Good," I say. "Really good." I open my backpack and read my *Romeo and Juliet* notes. The next time I look up, we're at my house.

"See you in a bit," I say to Jed.

I walk in to find Mom reading the paper and Pepper asleep under the kitchen table. The house looks nice. The blinds are all open and the furniture is shiny. "You dusted!" I say. I feel like doing a cartwheel because this must mean she feels better. I kiss her cheek and tell her that Toughie is doing well.

"Good," she says, smiling.

I run upstairs to my room and throw my backpack onto the bed. My room is dusted, too! Nail polish bottles are lined up neatly on my dresser and Mom's silver hairbrush is next to them. There's a note tied around it with a ribbon: *For my sweet Lily. You're the third generation to have this. I hope you treasure it as much as I treasure you. Love, Mom.*

It smells like baby powder. I choke back tears and almost run downstairs and give it back to her, but I can't. I set it down gently and go scrub my face instead.

When I go back to the kitchen, Jed's there, pouring a round of iced tea.

I lean over Mom's chair and hug her from behind. "Thank you for the hairbrush. I've always loved it."

She reaches up and pats my face. "You're welcome."

I smooth my tank top. "Feel like soup and sandwiches?"

"Let me help," Jed says, and stands.

Mom pulls him back down. "You sit." She smiles and winks. "How about...spaghetti?"

Spaghetti? I shove my fist onto my hip. "It's too hot for spaghetti. What else do we have?" I open the refrigerator and gasp. A plate full of neatly stacked sandwiches sits on the middle shelf. "Mom! You really should've been resting."

She turns to me and grins. "I'm allowed to do mom-type things. I can still handle microwaving bacon and cutting tomatoes. Plus, I figured you'd be pooped, too." She rubs my forearm and gives it a pat.

I grab the platter, set it on the table along with a jar of pickles, and kiss her ear. I realize that being able to do a little cooking or housework makes her feel good on the inside. I just wish it didn't make her hurt so much on the outside. "Thanks, Mom."

"Go ride, Lily," Jed says. He goes to the cupboard. "I'll get the rest." He winks at me and motions to the back of Mom's head. I take it as his signal that he's going to talk to Mom about being our helper.

I hesitate for a moment and watch Jed put out plates and a bag of chips.

"GO!" Mom shouts, poking me in the butt with her cane.

"Okay, okay." I grab half a sandwich, a can of soda and four carrots. I'm halfway down the porch steps when I stop, and then creep back to listen through the air conditioner in the window. As long as it's off for the moment, I'm able to hear them perfectly.

There's clinking and rustling before Jed finally clears his throat. "Listen, Sophia. I'm sure with all of Toughie's care, I'm going to owe you a small fortune. I was hoping I could pay it off by helping around here this summer."

I press my ear to the metal vent and give Jed's approach a thumbs-up. *Nice!*

"You know," he continues, "I could run errands, shop, help with the farm and the clinic. I'm very handy, too. I can fix anything."

He wasn't kidding about his sales ability. I cross my fingers and hope Mom buys it. I resist the urge to peek in the window when I hear Mom say, "You don't have to." She pauses and coughs. "I won't charge you, though."

I sink to the porch floor. It figures. She would just wipe his vet bills clean. She's just too kind.

Jed pipes in again. "It'd be good for me. I like to stay busy. I'm offering my summer services and I thought I'd offer them to you first." I hear his knuckles pop. "You know, it'd be good for Lily, too."

Without even seeing her, I know Mom's face just went soft. "Okay," I hear her say. "But... I'll tell Lily it was... my idea."

The legs of a chair squeak against the tile floor. I hear coffee cups clink and the sound of pouring before the aroma of java wafts through the air conditioner.

Mom finishes her thoughts. "I don't want Lily thinking... that you feel sorry... for us." She wheezes. "That's the deal."

The air conditioner rumbles and fires up. It blasts me with musty air and cuts my eavesdropping session short.

I hold my soda and sandwich with one hand and the carrots with the other. I pump my arms as I run toward the pasture.

I'm breathless when I offer Twilight a carrot. "Don't be mad. I got here as soon as I could."

He stomps his hind foot and switches his tail.

I climb onto the fence rail and pop my soda. "Come on, Twilight. Who's my buddy?"

He turns his hind end to face me and yanks a hunk of grass to chew.

"Fine." I throw the carrot within his reach and eat my sandwich.

The sun sinks into the treetops and a light breeze brings the scent of rain. I hear Pepper's stranger-is-here bark coming from the house. When she stops, I figure she got a whiff of a coon.

Twilight crunches the carrot and comes to me for more.

"Here you go, sweetlips."

"Are you talking to me or your horse?"

I swivel around to see Trent standing behind me. "To Twilight," I say, and turn back. I feel my face flush. I hardly ever see Trent outside of school anymore, so I'm the one surprised to see him this time. Especially without Emily.

There's an awkward silence for a minute until Trent reaches over the fence to Twilight and snaps his fingers. "Can I feed him one?"

I offer him a carrot as he plants himself on the top rail. "Be careful," I warn.

Twilight sniffs Trent's carrot and takes it between his teeth. He pulls, but doesn't bite through it. He tugs again.

Trent tugs back and laughs. "He's like a dog."

I just sit and watch quietly.

As Trent tugs again, Twilight bites through the carrot, sending Trent tumbling backwards and onto the grass.

I laugh as Trent brushes himself off. "Are you okay?" I stop myself from hopping off the fence and rushing to him.

He lifts an eyebrow. "You knew that was going to happen, didn't you?" He tosses the other half of the carrot near Twilight and rests his hands on the fence.

His fingernails are so clean and trimmed, I wonder if they've ever been in soil or grime. I shove my hands under my thighs. "So, what are you doing here?"

He rubs his palms together and kicks at the fence post with the tip of his boot. "I need you to look at Rocky. I think he's sick."

Now I get it. The reason for his presence becomes crystal clear. I'm his vet-girl-to-the-rescue. Never mind the fact we've known each other since kindergarten. That neighborly friendship ended for more reason than one several years ago. I hop off the fence and feed Twilight the last carrot. "I can't." I look him in the eyes. "I'm sorry. I have to take care of Twilight. He needs to ride," I tell him.

I skip telling him that I need my fix, too. That I've been yearning to get on Twilight and take off but I've been too busy the past four days. And four years.

Trent hops the railing and scratches Twilight on the nose. He seems oblivious to my irritation and asks, "Tomorrow then?"

"Look, Trent, I care about your horse, but I don't think I can handle seeing your dad." He takes a step back when I continue. "Plus, I haven't heard boo from you in how long, and now you show up asking for my help? You were the one who stopped being my friend thanks to Emily, remember?"

He stares at me for a few seconds before shoving his hands in his pockets. "That's not an issue anymore. When I waved at you and Jed yesterday, I was actually driving her home after breaking up with her."

My heart skips a beat. "And?" I say nonchalantly. "I'm not sure why I'm supposed to care about any of this."

"The thing is…" He pauses and rubs his collar bone. "When I told her about my plan to ask you to look at Rocky, she threatened to break up with me if I did. I've had it with that shit, so I broke it off with her."

I'm not sure if I should be pissed or flattered. Pissed at Emily for being so neurotic, or flattered that Trent kind of stood up for me. A little huff-laugh escapes me.

"So you've finally grown up just when Rocky needs my help. Convenient."

I can't keep myself from being harsh. Then it dawns on me why Emily gave me that near-miss scare with her car. She's up to her same old crap. Four years ago we were all friends. Trent, Emily, Shauna, and me. Trent and I had the longest history, since we'd been buddies as five-year-olds. All that changed in sixth grade when Emily became boy crazy and wanted Trent all to herself.

It's said that bad things happen in threes, and I definitely can't argue with that. My world spun out of control when Dad was fatally injured that same year. At a time when I needed friends most, I became an outsider. Like my sadness was catchy. Trent did whatever Emily said, and followed her like a puppy chasing liver sausage. Even Shauna and I saw less and less of one another. I drifted away from everyone except Mom. Bad thing number three was watching her MS get worse.

"Rocky needs your help because you're pretty much the town vet," Trent says calmly. "I thought I'd ask you instead of your mom." He motions to the house. "Should I ask her instead?"

"No, no," I stammer. I sigh and give in. "I'll come, but only if your dad isn't going to be there."

"Don't worry, you won't see him." Trent smiles. "Should I pick you up about ten tomorrow?"

I signal for Twilight to get low and I climb onto his back. "No. I'll ride Twilight over. He'll like that."

Trent backs up and hops over the fence. "See you then."

I click my tongue and Twilight begins to trot. I get into his rhythm as we cut through the tall grass. Swallows swoop around us. They zoom behind Twilight and over my head, catching all the bugs we kick up.

The moon rising over Beacon Hill is almost full. As we head toward the far end of our land, I hear Pepper's bark again. I see the glow of Trent's taillights backing out of the drive and onto Half Mile road.

I give Twilight a gentle nudge. His canter accelerates into a full run. A rush fills me. I grip his mane and squeeze my legs around him.

As we run the along the fence line at Half Mile road, Trent's headlights appear. He speeds up and we race, side by side, until Twilight slows to a trot.

Trent honks and sticks his head out the window. His thick hair whips around his face. "Until tomorrow."

My throat is so parched, it burns when I swallow. I wave before turning Twilight toward home. "Mom may not be too thrilled about this," I whisper. My heart pounds against my chest. I can't help the tiny bit of excitement that's welled up inside me. Seeing Trent has always made me smile. So I do.

Mosquitoes buzz my head as I say good night to Twilight. He switches his tail. I shake my hair and swat the air. My hand grazes a large spider web glued to the door frame of Twilight's stall.

The web is loaded with mosquitoes. "Bon appetite, Ms. Spidey," I say and take off toward the house.

The faster I run, the hotter I get. The hotter I get, the more my heat attracts those little blood-sucking buzzards.

A moth bounces on the porch light as I leap up the stairs and hurl myself into the kitchen. The house is quiet. Pepper doesn't bother to get up. She lifts her head, thumps her tail a few times, and sighs.

I'm relieved to see that the kitchen's clean. All I can think about is a cool shower and my bed. I peer out the window and look for Jed's truck. It's gone.

"Mom?" I unsnap my overalls and let them slide off me. I shuffle through the dining room with the buckles jingling like coins hitting the wood floor.

Mom closes her book when I peek into her room. "Long day," she says.

I stand in front of her air conditioner, letting the cold air make waves on my tank top and underwear. "Ahhh."

She clears her throat and motions for me to come closer and sit. "I want to talk to you … about Jed."

I crawl onto the foot of her bed, lie on my side and raise my arms over my head. I know what's coming but try to remain oblivious. "What about Jed?"

"I asked him to work … this summer. He needs our help." She takes a deep breath and fans herself. "And we need his. He liked my idea."

I nod, pretending this is all news to me. "I think it's a great idea," I say, even though I'm thinking, *my idea!* I ask questions even though I already know the answers. "Is he doing this for free? We can't afford to pay him."

Mom rests her palm on her cheek and wrinkles her chin. "Free vet care in exchange … " She swallows hard and reaches for her water. "Plus he agreed to . . . help me sell the Harley."

At that, I bolt upright. "What?" I must've missed that part of their conversation. "No, we should keep it."

She smiles and nods while rubbing the back of my hand. "It's okay."

Now I swallow hard. I rub her hand back. "Oh, Mom. Are you sure?"

She reaches for a photo on her side table and traces the outline of my dad on his Hog. "It's time," she whispers.

In my head, I know she's right, but my gut gets a sick feeling in it. A chunk of my heart just landed there.

"He was a . . . good man." She strokes the photo of him and me holding hands. "And a good father."

I rub my palm and remember his warm, gentle grip and how we'd swung our arms in harmony and giggled. After we had posed, he tossed me into the air and set me on his shoulders. Mom held his hand while we walked the county fairgrounds and shopped the horse auction. It was the best birthday I ever had. Eight years old, eight feet tall, and finding Twilight.

Mom kisses his face before placing the frame back in its spot. "It's time," she says again, but in a more matter-of-fact tone this time. Her chest heaves and she stares into space.

Another chunk of my heart somersaults into my gut. She's not talking about just selling the Harley now.

I see it in her faraway eyes. She's talking about being with him again. I hear it in her soft words as they coo, like a mourning dove, delivering sad and inevitable news. I feel it in the tender stroke she gives my cheek with her trembling fingers. She's talking about joining him, reuniting their souls.

Like burnt coffee with three heaps of sugar, the whole thing is bittersweet. I choke down the news but can't seem to swallow the lump left in my throat. *What's going to happen to me?*

Four

"Mom?" I whisper.

She hums a response and rolls onto her side.

"Dad would understand about the Harley." I climb off her bed and pull the sheets over her. "He'd want us to sell it if it means making it easier for you. For us."

Her breathing is steady and deep.

I kiss her temple. "Love you. Night."

As I scoop my jeans off the dining room floor, a pebble escapes from unknown parts and skips across the bare wood. Pepper chases it, eats it, and sniffs her way back to Mom's room.

I head upstairs, crush the jeans into the hamper, and run a cool shower. *Nice jeans, hillbilly.* Betsy's words soak into my head as I lather my hair. I wince, unable to control my imagination from directing the scene differently.

"Thanks," I say, as if she's said it as a compliment. Emily opens the door and I crawl into the back seat, where Shauna greets me with a high five. "Where're we heading?" I ask.

Emily's eyes meet mine in the rearview mirror. The way they're squinting lets me know she's smiling. "Miller's Pond for a dip."

We park near the weeping willow and pile out of the car. Then suddenly, we're twelve again. Giggly, innocent, long-legs twelve and racing to the water.

I flip off the shower and towel-dry my hair as I go to my dresser mirror. "Dreamer," I say to the chestnut eyes staring back at me. Then I glance at my bulletin board littered with photos. I straighten a photo of Emily, Shauna, and me. "Those days are gone."

My hair is exactly the same color in the picture as it is now. Sandy brown. I pull it into pigtails just like in the photo. Emily's blue eyes sparkle as Shauna gives a peace sign. They look pale in comparison to my summer tan.

The men's extra-large tank top sweeps my upper thighs before it settles on me. *Gray looks good on me.* I dab a droplet of four-year-old Brut on the shoulder seam. I soak in the scent, close my eyes, and imagine the purr of his Harley. "I miss you, Pop."

Pepper arrives at the doorway and harrumphs. Her big brown eyes are droopy. She wags her tail to one side when I reach for her. "Time for bed."

The ceiling fan dries my hair and blows her black coat as we claim our territories on my big bed. The Brut swirls in the air, bringing back childhood memories. Pepper licks my feet in a slow, soothing, trancelike motion. Weirdo.

Five hours of sleep later, I stagger to my window and scan the pasture. Saturday is muck day and I know I better get out there early, before it gets too hot. There's nothing worse than scooping horse crap out of the stall when it's ninety degrees.

Twilight rubs his teeth on the fence post and watches me from the pasture. He knows the routine. Crap removal, hose the stall, and lay fresh hay before breakfast. His and mine. He neighs and bobs his head as I cut the twine and loosen the hay.

"We'll go for a ride in a little bit." I smooth his mane before I leave him in his stall to munch.

With a push of my shoulder, I open the garage door and glance at the Harley. It's hidden under musty drop cloths and dust. I peek at the sidecar underneath and bite my lip. "It's time," I whisper and rub my old sparkly black helmet before I replace the drop cloths.

Pepper barks when I approach the porch and begin to peel off my boots. "Shhhh!" I hiss to her. "Mom's sleeping!" She quiets and presses her nose against the screen door.

"I'm up," Mom says from inside the kitchen.

She smiles when I poke my head into the room. "Good morning." I say. "Iced coffee looks good!"

"Close the door ... and turn on the air," she says, filling two glasses with ice. Her hands tremble until she sets the glasses down. She plucks a cube from her glass and rubs it on her wrist. Pepper's all bug-eyed, waiting for Mom to toss it to her. When she does, Pepper devours it in two seconds.

"It's going to be a hot one again today." The air conditioner rumbles before blowing cool air into the kitchen. It spits a couple of dust balls and settles into a steady hum. "I'm going to ride Twilight before it gets too hot." I guzzle half of my iced coffee and wipe my chin. "How about some toast before I go?"

Mom nods and sips her drink. It dribbles off the rim and drips onto her shirt. "Damn it!" She shakes her head in disgust and reaches to the center of the table. "Hand me a straw."

I obey and try to find the right words to talk to her about Trent. My gut flip-flops as I let out a sigh. "Mom?" I press the lever and the toaster's innards begin to glow. "Trent asked me for a favor."

She sets her glass down and raises an eyebrow.

I stand beside her and rub my neck. "Something's wrong with Rocky. He's sick and Trent wants me to check him over." I flinch when the toast pops up. Mom grins.

"I won't do anything but look at him, I promise," I say as I set the toast in front of her and sit down. "I told him I won't go if his dad is there. But if you don't want me to go at all, I won't."

Pepper drools as Mom folds her toast. "Tell Trent hello ... from me." She sops up the melted butter and nibbles the corner.

I kiss her on the cheek. "Thank you, Mom. I didn't want to sneak and do it without you knowing where I was."

"You don't have to sneak!" She laughs and pats my hand. "Dr. Collins and I may not be friendly ... " She clears her throat and takes a sip of coffee. "But that doesn't mean you and Trent can't be."

"It's not like that," I say. "I just thought you should know where to find me in case there's an emergency or you need me."

She cuts me off. "I'll be fine." She pulls herself up and shuffles to the sink. "You go on." She wiggles her eyebrows, making me laugh.

"I'll be home before lunch."

After I scarf my toast and change out of my crap clothes, I head to the barn and saddle up Twilight. "Such a good boy you are," I say, checking the stirrups. As I settle onto him, a quiver under his mane erupts and rolls like a wave down his back. He can hardly contain himself, he's so excited. "Take it easy." I smile and give him a light nudge with the heel of my boot.

We trot toward the house, then down the driveway to the trail alongside the road. I ease up on the reins to signal he can let loose. We give the trail a beating and fly. "Go Twi, go!"

The mid-morning sun dries the sweat on my face as we ease to a gentle walk and enter Trent's homestead. His dog, Elmo, barks incessantly and bounds toward us, his upper lip curling to reveal tiny teeth.

"Oh, hush, Elmo!" I slide off Twilight and bend to greet the old boy. "For a little schnauzer, you're a good watch dog." He sniffs my palm and wags his tail, but then turns and growls at Twilight.

Trent pops out from under his pickup. "Hey! You're here!" He snaps his fingers and pats his chest. Elmo runs a few steps and leaps into his arms. "He's an old crab but he couldn't bite a pimple off your ass. Ah ... " He pauses. "Make that *my* ass."

"Anyone's ass." I crack up and notice him blushing. I wonder if he's blushing because he mentioned my ass, or if it's because he swore. I opt for the latter. "It's okay, Trent. I say *ass* too."

He smiles and cracks his neck before gently tossing Elmo onto the grass. "You can tie Twilight up over there." He raises his chin to signal where to go.

We walk the gravel driveway to a tie-post in the shade and I try to make small talk while removing supplies from my saddle bag. "What is Elmo, about ten now?"

Trent fills a barrel of water for Twilight and wets his blond hair. He laughs as he slicks it back. "Yep. He turned ten when I turned sixteen. Got him for my sixth birthday." He states it so proudly, he's practically beaming.

My forehead tightens as I look at him sideways. He seems nervous. I find it amusing and kind of cute. "I know, Trent. I was there, remember?"

He takes my elbow and leads me across the yard to the stables. "I remember."

"You had an Elmo birthday cake and *Sesame Street* plates and napkins." I sigh and giggle. "I was so jealous you got a puppy as a gift!"

"And here I am, sixteen with an old dog named Elmo! Why didn't I pick Duke or Butch or something…"

"Less girlie?" I crack up and he raises an eyebrow.

"Less childish." He gives me a playful evil eye.

I untie the bandana from around my forehead and wipe my face. "It's all in the way you say it." I clear my throat. "El*mo* sounds way more manly than *El*mo."

Trent laughs and curls his arms like a body builder. "El*mo*! El*mo*!" Then he pulls the stable door open and swings one arm, motioning me to go first.

Rocky stands quietly in his stall as I greet him. "Hi, Rock. How ya doing?"

I take his chart off the wall and scan his feeding schedule. "So, what has he been acting like or doing to make you think he's sick?"

"For one, he's been lying down more than usual, and he stands different, like he's getting ready to pee."

I enter the stall and set my bag on the ledge. I peel back Rocky's lips. "His gums look good. Have you been riding him?"

Trent kicks the dirt floor and shakes his head. "Not as much as I should. Ever since I got my truck, it's been hard."

"Ah." I roll my eyes. I slide my hand down Rocky's leg and check for a pulse. "So far, so good." I check Rocky for sores and then listen to his belly. "He sounds a little gassy. I have peppermint leaves in my bag there." I lift my chin toward the ledge. "Mix those in with his next meal and that'll help sooth his gut."

Trent pulls out the bag of leaves, sniffs them, and watches me push my thumbs near Rocky's cheekbones. "I'm applying acupressure on areas that affect the digestive system," I explain.

"Okay." Trent looks skeptical. "Does that really work?"

"It's been around a long time. Mom used to do full acupuncture but switched to acupressure when her tremors got bad." I rub Rocky's mane. "Good boy." I bend and examine a fresh pile of crap. "Have his stools been normal?"

Trent shrugs. "He's going as much as normal, I guess. Our horse handler, Max, cleans the stalls, so we should ask him."

I sigh and take Rocky's reins. "This is *your* horse, Trent. Take care of him already! Let's let him roam the field while we talk to Max."

Before we're out of the stable, Rocky raises his tail and craps three large piles. I take a closer look as Trent backs away. "No visible worms. Good." I shake my head and take joy in the pruned-up look on Trent's face.

We interrupt Max and another worker busy laying bricks for a new patio. Max offers us bottled water from his cooler and I guzzle half of mine immediately.

"Rocky's been acting funny for about a week," Max tells me. His rich Spanish accent is charming. "He seems, how do you say, depressed?"

I smile and hold the cold water bottle to my neck. "He could be. What about his food intake? Has that changed? Is he eating more or less?"

Max whispers something to the other worker and shoos him away. "He seems to like the new grain. He's eating the same amount."

I shoot a glare at Trent. "New grain? Did you know about this?"

"Not really."

"Okay, Max," I say, stepping closer to him. "Rocky needs to go back on the grain he was on before he started acting funny. Starting today, mix half of his old feed with half of his new feed. Add a little less new feed everyday until he's back on his old feed one hundred percent."

Max nods. "I understand."

I grab Trent's shoulder, "And Trent is going to ride him *every day*." I squint at Trent. "Your workers will not do that for you. Okay?"

"I'll try."

I thank Max and turn to go, but he stops me. "*Senorita?*" he says, so sweetly it sends chills up my sweaty neck.

"Yes?" I say.

The other worker appears and extends a frosty bunch of red grapes. "They are straight from the freezer. They will cool you down and quench your hunger," Max tells me.

"Frozen grapes?" I grin, take the bunch, and pop one into my mouth. "It's like a little scoop of sherbert! Thank you."

Trent plucks a couple from my bunch as we walk away. I turn to Max and shout, "Rocky pooped in the stable, but Trent said he'll clean it up!"

"*Gracias*, Trent," Max calls.

"Thanks a lot, Lily!" Trent grabs the bunch of grapes and walks stiff-legged to the stable. I follow and try to snatch it back, but he blocks me at every grab. "Okay. I'll share if you help me clean the poop," he says.

"Let's eat first." I slide my back down the door frame and sit on the floor. "I think Rocky has a bit of stomach trouble. Once he's back on a regular exercise routine and his normal diet, he should bounce back. If he doesn't, we'll have to check for colic."

Trent frowns. "I'll ride him tomorrow," he says, digging his heels into the dirt.

The flies begin to buzz us and go for the grapes. I hear Twilight neigh as I stand and wipe my hands on my back pockets. "Colic is no joke. It really can be serious, so take it easy on him tomorrow. Don't let him get overheated."

Trent leans out the doorway and watches Rocky in the pasture. "How serious? Like, he'd have to be put down?" He turns to me with his eyebrows in a knot.

"If it's advanced, there's nothing else you can do. There's no cure." A lump forms in my throat. I swallow hard and swig some water. "It'd be inhumane and cruel to let him suffer."

Trent grabs a shovel and scoops a pile. "I don't want him to suffer."

"I know." My nose tingles and I clench my jaw. "I have to go."

"Hey!" He follows me over to Twilight and lays his hand on my boot after I swing up into the saddle. "But you said you'd help."

"I'm helping by having you do it all by yourself. Believe me." My tone is a little more biting than he deserves. "You can't have other people always doing your stuff for you. Fend for yourself once in a while."

"Sheesh." He holds his palms out and backs away. "Where'd this come from?"

"I have my own crap to shovel, that's where it comes from. And a whole lot more." I steer Twilight away from the water barrel, my hand on my chest as I try not to cry. "I'm sorry, Trent. Really. I guess I'm jealous again. And it's not about Elmo this time. I wish I had your *problems*."

He nods his head and blinks knowingly. "Want to ride tomorrow morning?" He steps closer and strokes Twilight's neck. "Get out for an hour? I'll bring grapes," he singsongs, and raises an eyebrow.

I tilt my head. "Sure. I guess so."

"Meet halfway? Near the old grain silo?" He walks alongside Twilight as we head to the trail.

I nod. "Around seven thirty?" I nudge Twilight down the gully as Trent leans against his mailbox. "I'm sorry about biting your head off," I call as we begin to trot away.

"Don't worry about it." He flips his bangs and smiles. "See you at seven thirty."

I give him a thumbs-up. I take it slow on the trail and try to enjoy the warm breeze and birdcalls. A burning in my gut competes with a lump in my throat. "It isn't an official date, is it Twi?" As if on cue, Twilight snorts and whips his tail. "I hope not, too," I tell him.

Five

I yank Twilight to a halt when we reach the edge of Jed's driveway. "That wasn't here this morning." I scan the property and sigh. "Now what?" Tears cloud my vision as we pass the *For Sale* sign.

Jed putting his house up for sale, the day after he agreed to help us, worries me. My jaw clenches. I wish I could take it all back and forget ever asking him. This makes our whole arrangement feel just a little too permanent. My heart sinking with dread, I click my tongue and urge Twilight to top velocity. He stomps the tall grass as we speed away from Jed's farm.

We run full-out until I see Jed's truck parked near my house. I hop off Twilight and walk him slowly toward the barn. He pulls me to the water barrel and sucks in a gallon while I take off the saddle and blanket. "That's a good boy. You cool down now." I let him into the pasture to graze, and take off my boots and socks.

Pepper kicks a cloud of dust as she runs down the road to greet me. Her butt knocks into my knees as she spins. She grabs a sticky sock and prances toward the house.

I wipe my face with my bandana and follow her. Mom and Jed have lunch spread on the table as I enter.

"What is going on here?" I hold back tears and tilt my head. Puddles of sunlight glisten on the tile floor, reflecting into my eyes. The wall clock ticks, keeping time with a booming inside my chest. *Tick tick.*

They stop loading their crackers with cheese and sausage and share a look.

"Have a seat," Mom says, patting the chair beside her.

"I don't want to sit down, Mom. I want you to tell me what is going on." I take a deep breath. "I just went by your house, Jed. There's a *For Sale* sign on the lawn." I reach for a chair and grip its back. My hands stop trembling.

Jed pushes his plate away and folds his hands. *Tock tock.*

"The two of you are sitting here casually having lunch and discussing, what?" My knuckles whiten as I squeeze the chair. "Whatever it is affects me, and I deserve to know what the hell is going on."

Mom's eyes widen. "Sit down, Lily." She reaches for me as I slide into the chair. "You're right. It does affect you. I think it would be better ... if Jed lives here."

I shake my head and take in her words. "Lives here? Like for good?" I eye Jed. "And you agreed to this?" I want to shout, *No, you can't move in! It'll make it too easy for her to give up.*

"I've been thinking about selling my place anyway. It's too much for one man."

Words shoot out of me. "When I asked you to come help us, I didn't mean move in," I huff. I wipe my hands down my face and stare at Jed. My jaw aches. "Thanks a lot."

Mom looks at Jed, then at me. "You asked him?"

"She did." Jed folds his napkin. "It was a mutual decision that the idea come from me."

Mom just nods. Wrinkles appear in her forehead.

Jed cracks his knuckles and leans forward. "All this means is that you'll be able to live here forever, Lily."

I glance at Mom. "Forever?" This has got to be all her idea. She's making sure I'm taken care of. I keep a poker face and wait for her to respond.

Jed speaks up when she looks away. "I'll stay as long as your Mom needs me, or until you're eighteen."

A vision of Jed and me sitting quietly on the porch invades my thoughts. *This is bullshit.* "Didn't either of you think about asking what I thought about this? You just went ahead and made plans and put the farm up for sale? What if I don't want to stay here?" The pulse in my neck quickens at the thought of being in this house alone.

They're silent. Wearing matching expressions of disbelief.

I throw my hands up and let them slap my sides. "Where will you go when I'm eighteen, huh?" I say to Jed. "Have you thought of that?"

Jed shakes his head. "I haven't thought that far ahead, but maybe down South or just into town somewhere. What's important to your mom is you staying at home, no matter what. And I agree."

"No matter what ... happens to me," Mom says softly before kissing my palm.

I knew it. Having someone here to watch over me is the ace in her hand. "Stop. Stop talking like that." I kneel next to her. "With Jed's help, we'll be able to take proper care of you from now on." I can hardly breathe, I'm talking so fast. "If having him live here means you'll be here longer ... " I nod at her, hoping she'll agree, "I'm all for it."

She presses her lips together and blinks. The nod I'm waiting for doesn't come. "Please!" I beg. "Jed coming here was supposed to make it easier for you to live, not to let go."

She runs her fingers through my hair and cups my chin. "Like a daylily ... we'll take it one day at a time."

My tears soak her thin skin. I'm sick to my stomach with guilt. My idea to have Jed help us isn't turning out as planned. Mom just upped the ante. Jed being so agreeable wasn't supposed to be part of the deal. His friendship is both a blessing and a curse right now.

"When will he move in?" I whisper. I don't want to hear the answer, but I have to know. The closer it gets to him living here, the closer it gets to me losing her.

The room becomes still. Quiet. And I wonder if it's just me or if the clock really has become louder. I rub my temple.

"A couple of weeks," Mom says. "Once school is over."

"And my driving route, too." Jed smiles and builds a cheese-and-sausage tower on a cracker. I want to shove it down his throat for acting so casual. Then he adds, "We'll start bringing the animals over next week."

Next week. I straighten and let go of Mom's hand, wiping my face and forcing a smile even though my insides are ripping apart. "Your birthday is next week," I say softly. I swallow the lump in my throat and try to think of cake and singing. For her.

"You'll be nifty fifty. Right, Sophia?" Cracker crumbs spill out of Jed's mouth as he speaks.

"Yes. Nifty fifty. " Mom laughs. "And you're ... super sixty, Jed."

I stand up and go look at the calendar. "Fifty is a biggie," I say, and immediately feel like an idiot. Every birthday is a biggie for someone who wants to die. I push away thoughts of our uncertain future and try to focus on her special day. I allow myself to look forward one week. "I'll make a nice dinner and we'll have a party."

Pepper bounds from her rock collection and splashes in the sun puddle at my feet.

"Yes, Pep, a party!" I say and laugh weakly. "How about pork ribs, roasted corn, and a chocolate cake?"

Jed rubs his stomach. "As long as Pisser, Sunbeam, and Mama Sow don't get mad at me, sign me up!"

Mom squints. "Oh, Jed … you're too much." She smiles at me. "That sounds good … Lily." Her hazel eyes pour love into mine so I soak it in, not blinking, till she breaks her gaze.

I offer a round of iced tea and sit again. As frustrated as I am about Jed moving in, I know he's doing it for Mom. This turn of events has ripped a hole in my heart and it hurts. But I'm spent, and too tired to hold a grudge. "How is Toughie, Jed? Better, I hope."

He chews for a moment and says, "He seems fine, Lily. You're a skilled vet tech."

Mom nods and winks at me. "And how's Rocky?"

I sigh and build a cracker. "All his vitals are good, but there's weird bowel sounds even though his crap looks normal." I pick at the cracker as Pepper begs at my feet. "The stable hand changed his feed, so I told him to wean the old food back into his diet."

"Good," Mom says.

"Stable hand?" Jed snorts. "Must be rough."

I roll my eyes. "I know. I also told Trent he has to ride Rocky every day." I flip a cracker to Pepper to stop her from drooling on my leg. "So, we're going riding tomorrow morning."

"Ahhh," Mom says and raises her chin.

I feel my face flush and hold my cold glass to my forehead. "No, Mom. It's just a ride. As old friends."

She smirks. "Then why are . . . you blushing?"

"I'm not blushing," I say, but I know I am. I suddenly feel frazzled and under the spotlight. I wipe sweat off my nose. "It's boiling hot in here. Plus, I've known Trent forever. We're just friends." I guzzle my tea in an attempt to shut down the topic.

Mom and Jed share a look. "Friends are good," Jed says with a wide grin.

Scenes of Dad and Jed flash in my brain. Their boisterous laughter and popping beer cans fill me as I gather crumbs and swipe them onto my napkin. I ache for the old days but blink away the thoughts. I put my game face on. "I have a huge end-of-the-year report due. I need to do homework."

Jed clears his place and takes Mom's dishes. Mom winks at me. "Thank you for asking for . . . Jed's help."

I give her a little *you're welcome* nod but inside I'm chastising myself. *Way to go, stupid! Your bright idea backfired. Jed was supposed to help Mom. Help her feel better, not help her let go. He was supposed to be here to take care of her. Not of me.*

I clean the table before trudging up to my room. It's stuffy. I pound the corners of the window frame before sliding it open. Yellow paint chips crumble into the sill. I fan fresh air into the room, flop onto my bed, and stare at my pile of books.

I breathe in deep, scribbling a few sentences for my book report on *Romeo and Juliet*: *Juliet fakes her death using a sleeping potion and waits for Romeo. Romeo never received word that her death is an act to fool their families, and when he finds her, he believes she is really dead. Romeo drinks a bottle of poison and kills himself in despair. Juliet wakens from her deep sleep and finds Romeo dead. She tries to drink any remaining poison from the vial and when that fails, she kisses him, hoping there's enough poison left on his lips. Ultimately, she decides his dagger would be a faster death. Their love was so strong, they'd rather die than live unhappy.*

From the white pine outside my window, a male cardinal calls for a mate. Over and over it sings. I listen and imagine him repeating, "Ju-li-et, Ju-li-et."

I erase my last word and replace it with *apart*.

I go to the window and watch the cardinal hop from branch to branch. "Being apart doesn't mean being unhappy. You have to go on without her," I whisper.

Mom calls my name and I practically fly to the top of the stairs. "What is it, Mom?"

"Phone for you," she says, and sets it on the bottom step.

"Oh, thanks." I relax my shoulders. I ride the banister and land hard before picking up the phone. "Hello?"

"Hey, Lily. It's Shauna." She clears her throat. "Listen, we have that big report due on Tuesday and I forgot my book at school."

"Again?" I say in a perturbed tone. This is so typical of Shauna. Last semester, she needed my Ethics textbook and notes so I met her at the library. Last year she accidently deleted our entire PowerPoint for Spanish class and I had to redo it alone.

"And I was hoping I could borrow your book. Are you done with it?"

I bite my lip and sit on the stair. "No. I'm still using it to finish up. I'm almost done though."

I hear a big sigh on her end. "Shoot. I want to work on it today since I have to go to a wedding all day tomorrow."

"No one else in class can loan it to you?" I try not to sound irritated. "I have plans tomorrow, too."

"Naw, I asked a couple people and they're either not doing it or are already done with it." She clears her throat. "Is it possible we could share it?"

I absorb her question before I ask, "How far along are you?"

Her voice becomes upbeat. "I just have to write the timeline and conclusion. That's it."

I smile and shake off my suspicion. No way would I let her plagiarize my report. "Okay. That's exactly where I am. Come on over and we'll share the book."

"I'll be over in twenty minutes."

When I enter the kitchen and hang up the phone, Mom and Jed look up from their crossword puzzle. "That was Shauna?" Mom asks.

"Yep. She's coming over to do homework."

Mom straightens and tilts her head. "Well, that's nice."

I shrug my shoulders. "I guess." I stop at the bottom stair and call into the kitchen, "Don't be shocked when you see her, Mom. She's kind of a goth chick now."

"Goth?" Mom says.

"Yeah. She wears all black and has spiked hair." I head upstairs and shout, "Send her up when she gets here."

I hear Mom tell Jed, "We called them ... punk rockers. I was more the hippie type."

Jed laughs and says, "What do you mean, *was*."

An image of Mama wearing fringed pants and little round sunglasses, riding on the back of Daddy's motorcycle, makes me grin. I turn on my old clock radio and clear the static. My choices are slim. Talk radio, country, or an oldies station. I settle for oldies.

The theme song from *Friends* pipes in and I step back. "What timing," I say. I pluck a photo off of my bulletin board and clench my teeth.

My stomach sizzles. Shauna, Emily, and I mug for the camera and show off our carved pumpkins. My carving spells *HAPPY*, Shauna's spells *BIRTH*, and Emily's spells *DAY*. We lit the pumpkins instead of a cake and ate warm chocolate pudding for my twelfth.

The DJ pipes in with "That was 'I'll Be There For You' by the Rembrandts." I sing the title mockingly. I flick Emily's face with my finger before I toss the photo into my underwear drawer. "Up until Dad died." I click off the radio, grab Mom's—my—hairbrush, and sigh. As I brush my hair into a tight ponytail and smooth out the bumps, I study my face and wonder why it seems like everyone else has changed except me. Puckering my lips, I imagine myself in all black, like Shauna. I giggle under my breath and turn away from the mirror. "Not a good look."

I'm straightening my comforter when Shauna steps into my room. "Hey," she says.

I gasp when I see her. "Wow." I look her up and down. Her brown hair falls straight around her face and her T-shirt and jeans actually fit her. The silver cross lies flat at her neckline. "You look... normal."

She laughs and throws her backpack onto my bed. "I didn't want to freak out your mom." She checks herself in my dresser mirror. "The goth thing is getting old anyway."

67

"After two years?" I ask, even though I totally agree.

She smoothes her T-shirt and leans against the dresser. "I hate getting up early. Spiking my hair, putting on make-up and earrings—it's a lot of work."

"Four holes is a lot." I grimace when I check out her ears. "And now you'll have lots of extra time...for homework."

"Sure," she says with a laugh. "Like that's my plan." She rubs her palms on her knees and looks around my room. "Man. This room brings back so many memories."

My cheeks get warm as I follow her gaze to my Breyer horse collection. "I'll never get rid of those. I don't care if they seem babyish," I snap.

"I think they're cool. I didn't say they were babyish."

The room gets quiet, except for the radio, as she continues to inspect my collection.

"It's nice you still have them." She goes to the shelf and rubs her finger across a stallion. "This one looks like Twilight."

I let out my breath and stretch my neck side to side. "He's my favorite one. It was from my dad."

Shauna stares and bites her lip. She sighs and crosses her arms. "Look, Lily, I don't want you thinking I came over here to use you for your book."

I shake my head. "Well, didn't you? I mean, it's not like we really hang out anymore. After Dad died, we went from best friends to school friends." I pick up

Romeo and Juliet and toss it onto my bed. "So let's just study."

Shauna sits on the windowsill and taps her foot. "All right. You're right." Her eyes are glued to the floor. "We may not be as close as we used to be, but I still think about you a lot." Her voice trails off in a quiver. "And the book gave me a good excuse to call you."

I sit on the corner of my bed. Silent. Stunned. I want to get up and hug her, but I don't. I grip the mattress and cement my feet to the floor. When she finally looks at me, I smile.

"Ah, shit, Lily." She throws her hands up. "When your dad died, you blamed the world. I didn't know how to help you."

"Well at least you didn't desert me completely." I give her that, because it's true. An occasional lunch together if we happened to be in the same line, being paired up on assignments in classes we shared, and of course, homework partners as needed.

As if she's reading my mind, she says, "I've been a pretty sucky friend."

"No, a truly sucky friend would've acted like I dropped off the face of the earth. That would be Emily." I sneer and cross my legs.

Shauna spins a silver stud in her ear and chews her bottom lip. "I'm not making excuses for her, but on top of wanting Trent to herself, I think she just couldn't deal with your grief. Keeping herself away made her feel safe."

I cock my head and squint at her. "Like death was catchy?"

"I'm not saying it was right, but I think it was her way of handling it." Shauna turns and looks out my window.

"Are you saying becoming a snot was her way of coping?" I laugh sarcastically and roll onto my side. "I'd be the biggest snot rag on the planet if that's how I coped."

She looks at me all serious. "We were twelve and stupid." She pauses and raises a hand. "Scratch that. I was stupid." She shakes her head. "And then when we got to high school, Emily and Trent were still an item and I fell for Blake and got into the whole goth scene." She rolls her eyes.

"Just be yourself, Shauna," I say. "Or is the 'whole goth scene' you?"

"It's seriously like Halloween everyday!" She laughs and lifts her bangs to a spike. "Besides, it's over. Blake just broke up with me at Sophomore Social."

"I'm sorry," I say and choke back what my mind really thinks. *Good! He's a creep and an A-hole!*

"I'll get over it," she says. "Hey, we should go to the all-school water fight on the last day of classes." She pauses and wriggles her eyebrows. "Just us girls!"

I push off the corner of my bed and clasp my hands behind my neck. That would be fun. I wonder if Trent would be there. The thought of going and being part of the high school crowd makes me instantly nervous and excited, but I can't bring myself to show it. "I'll have to see what's going on when it gets closer," I tell her. "Not that I don't want to or anything, I just don't have the same freedom you do. Believe me, I'd love to go."

She blinks and nods.

I quickly change the subject. "So, it seems that breaking up is going around."

Shauna plops onto my bed and sits cross-legged. "Really? Who else broke up?"

I go to my underwear drawer, pull out the old pumpkin photo, and toss it at her. "Emily and Trent."

Her face blanches when she looks at the picture of us. "Oh, wow, Emily and Trent? Hey, I remember this night!"

"Yeah, that was fun." I take the photo and seem to make Shauna happy by pinning it back up on my bulletin board.

"So why'd they break up? Do you know?" she asks.

I settle onto my bed, shuffle my homework papers, and click my pen. "No, but I'm sure I'll find out tomorrow. Trent and I are going riding."

Shauna's eyes widen and she nods slowly with a smirk. "Ahhh."

"No," I cut into her thoughts. "We're only friends."

"Yeah, but Emily will freak if she finds out."

I flip my wrist and shrug. "I don't have to explain anything to her. Let her think what she wants. It's totally crazy that I've seen both you and Trent today. After all these years..." I glance at the photo and sigh. "But like you said, things are different now."

"Yeah." Shauna shoves my shoulder with her fist. "And I'm glad I left my book at school this weekend."

"Me too," I say just as Pepper races into the room and jumps onto the bed. "Get down!" I yell, covering my papers.

Shauna lands on the floor and Pepper is all tongue on her. "Holy crap, this is Pepper?" She rolls and tries to deflect licks to her face.

Pepper flops onto her back and kicks her feet while squirming side to side. Her coat stinks of fish and her paws are wet.

"Eww, Pepper!" I cover my nose. "Get out!" I point to the hallway. She cowers and slinks by me. "Sorry," I say as I shut my door.

Shauna giggles and wipes off her face. "She was playful the last time I saw her. At least she hasn't changed much."

"That's true." A pang of guilt comes over me and I regret yelling at her. "Thank God for Pepper."

Six

After an hour of working on book reports, our grumbling stomachs lead us to the kitchen where Mom sits alone. "Jed left?" I ask, popping a bag of popcorn into the microwave.

Mom continues reading and just nods.

"Either of you want a soda?" I ask.

"Sure," Shauna says, plopping herself into a chair across from Mom.

Mom folds her newspaper and yawns. "No thanks. I need to lie down."

I stand behind her and rub her shoulders lightly. "Are you okay? Can I get you something?"

"I'm stiff. Help me ... to bed." She holds onto the table as she stands. She stops mid-turn and lets out a groan. I slide my arm around her waist.

Her face is pale and she seems frozen in to the floor. "Get my wheels."

I hurry around the table and pull the wheelchair from its spot in the corner of the dining room. I roll it next to Mom and lock the wheels.

Shauna's eyes meet mine. She looks at Mom, and then me again. "Can I help?" she asks, standing up.

"No, no," Mom says as I guide her into the seat. "I've been sitting ... too long. That's all."

I flip the lever to unlock the wheels and begin to roll Mom out of the kitchen. She brakes in front of Shauna and smiles. "It's good to ... see you again, Shauna."

Shauna slides back into her chair and faces Mom. "Good to see you too, Sophia."

Mom points to her bedroom. "Onward."

I push, and we're turning the corner just as the microwave buzzes. "I'll get the popcorn," Shauna shouts.

"Let me sleep ... for an hour," Mom says as I help her into bed. "We can order ... pizza tonight."

I pull the sheet to her chin. "That sounds good. I'll order so it's here when you wake up."

She winks and rubs my arm. "Shauna can stay, too."

I take a deep breath and look to the ceiling. "We'll see. I'll think about it."

I don't mention the pizza or anything about Mom when Shauna, Pepper, and I settle back in my room. Pepper stares, entranced, at the popcorn bowl as if she's willing it to her. As if tasting it with her eyes. I set a handful of popcorn on the carpet for her.

Shauna curls her legs under her and opens *Romeo and Juliet*. She flips through the chapters and without looking up says, "So your mom has gotten worse, huh?"

I study her face and watch her eyebrows twitch. When she looks at me I say, "Yeah. She's worse since the days when we hung out."

Her face pales and I immediately backpedal. "I didn't mean it like that. She started getting bad after Dad died. Then, worse after eighth grade graduation. There's no way you could've known, so don't feel bad. Like you said, we were stupid." When her color returns, I try to explain about Mom without getting too technical. "The multiple sclerosis has really damaged her nerves. It's running havoc throughout her entire system."

"Is there anything that will help her?"

"She was being treated by Trent's dad but she hated the drugs. They didn't work for her. After Dad died, the disease went into overdrive from stress. It was pretty awful. I thought I'd lose her, too."

"Dang." Shauna stares at me with this horrified expression. "I'm sorry you went through all that. I had no idea."

"Yeah, well, it's not like you could've done anything." I roll my eyes and let out a breath. "The last four years she's just used bee stings. And rest."

Shauna's neck stiffens. "Bee stings?" She shivers and wiggles as though a bug just crawled up her back. "That sounds painful. So she stings herself, or what?"

I huff and try not to seem annoyed, but I am. Shauna's right. I did blame the world when Dad died, and once again, I find it easy to blame the world for Mom's pain. I don't want to lash out but it's so, so hard not to. It's much easier to just not talk about it. Easy isn't always best, but I guess that's my way of coping. I grit my teeth and punch my thigh with the side of my fist.

Shauna's face loses all expression. "I'm sorry. I ask too many questions. I didn't mean to piss you off. I guess I'm making up for lost time, ya know?"

"It's not you." I hop off the bed and pace with my hands clutched on top of my head. "It's just that I don't talk to anyone about Mom."

"Not anyone?"

I stop pacing and look at her for a second. "That's what I just said." I stifle a laugh and grin at her. "You haven't changed a bit. A-million-questions Shauna."

She laughs and blushes. "I'm not trying to be nosy. Seriously. I have my mom's lawyer blood, I guess." She holds her palm up. "Tell me to back off and I will, but just so you know, you can talk to me like you used to."

I crawl back onto the bed and stuff a pillow onto my lap. "Well, thanks, I appreciate that. And if I do ever tell you anything, and I mean *anything*"—I raise my eyebrows and enunciate every syllable—"It. Is. Strictly. Between. Us."

"Of course," Shauna says. "You can trust me, Lily. Even after all this time."

I study my timeline of *Romeo and Juliet* and before I realize it's out of me, I blurt, "I sting Mom."

"Holy shit, Lily." Shauna reaches for my arm but I pull away.

"That's it. That's about it." I shrug and press my lips together. "Medicine wasn't working so bee venom therapy is what she wanted to use." I lower my eyes and pull a thread from the blanket. "Until now."

I twirl the thread around my finger several times, cutting off the circulation.

Shauna scoots toward me but doesn't say a word.

Maybe it's because she's probably the one person who knows me best, or maybe it's because she said I can trust her, but I feel the need to say it out loud to someone. So I spill about Mom.

"Mom told me she was ready to quit." I glance up to gauge Shauna's reaction.

She looks puzzled. "Quit the bee thing?"

"That's part of it." I wind the thread tighter. "She wants me to give her a higher dose of stings. The most she's ever had at one time is twelve, and that amount just isn't doing much for her anymore. She said if sixteen stings doesn't work, she wants to quit."

"And do what?" Her eyes grow wide.

I stare at my throbbing fingertip and shake my head. "Like I said, if it doesn't work, she's ready to quit." I keep my head bowed and look up at her.

Shauna puts her hand to her chest and takes a deep breath. "My God." She fingers the cross and rocks. "*Quit* quit? She can't do that. Why would she do that? To you!"

I snap the thread off my finger and lean back. "She's afraid she'll get so bad that she'll end up lingering on life support like my dad did." I pinch the bridge of my nose. A nervous laugh comes over me. "When he got trapped under the tractor, they did everything they could to save him. He was in a coma for a month before Mom decided to turn off the ventilator. Everyone said it's what he would've wanted, but I begged her not to. I begged her and I always wonder..."

Shauna points a finger at me. "Don't. Don't torture yourself like that. My God, blame the whole world if you have to, but don't blame yourself. You were a kid." She hesitates. "You know, there's a big difference between what happened to your dad and what your mom wants to do." She makes a little sign of the cross. "It's a sin, Lily. She shouldn't think that way."

Her words sink in and crawl under my skin. "It's not exactly the same, sure, but I wouldn't say there's a big difference," I say. "The only difference is that someone else made the decision for my dad. My mom wants that control for herself. I don't like, but I get it." I feel my eyes welling up and my cheeks getting warm.

"Even though I don't agree, I get it, too," Shauna says, bowing her head. "I got an A on an Ethics report about compassion. Having a lawyer for a mom was really helpful when I researched Oregon's Death with Dignity laws."

"Mom has a bunch of pamphlets about that," I say. "But she says that if you're not considered terminal, you don't have that luxury."

Shauna's eyes get wide. "Luxury? She actually said that?"

I nod and feel my chin tighten.

Shauna hugs me. "You know, my main point in my report was that physician-assisted suicide isn't a sin like regular sui—"

"Hey!" I cut her off. She pretends to lock her lips and throw away the key.

I press on my temples. The last thing I want to do is get into a debate about ethics and sin. I debate with myself enough as it is. For now, I decide not to tell Shauna that Mom asked me to let her go if our experimental dose of sixteen stings is too much. *Do not resuscitate.* My head is pounding. I open my folder and pass her my outline.

After we work for a few minutes, Shauna's foot starts twitching and I can tell she's dying to ask more questions. I change the subject by sticking my foot in my mouth. "So, you and Blake broke up, huh?"

She smiles. "Ah ha. See? Questions are conversation starters. You do it too, and you're not being nosy, are you?"

I wrinkle my face and stick out my tongue. "I guess." I slug her shoulder. "I didn't say you were nosy."

She pouts and says, "Blake broke up with me. He said he wants to be free this summer."

I decide to feel her out before I make any negative comments about Blake. "Okay, tell me to back off if you want, but were you guys serious?"

Her eyes go soft and she tilts her head, all dreamy. "I thought so."

"No," I say, snapping her out of la-la land. "I mean *serious.*" Beads of sweat form on her forehead as she senses that I'm going to give her a good grilling.

"Oh!" She gets all flustered and waves her hands. "No. We did not get *serious.*" She lifts a shoulder and pretends to be sexy. "Not that he didn't want to. I just wouldn't."

"Oh, good!" I blurt. "He's a creep and you could do so much better."

She shoots me an evil eye and shoves her hand on her hip. "That's a bit harsh."

I lean forward and hold up my hands. "Well, I'm sorry, but he rubs me the wrong way. He's got a reputation for being a badass and I worried every time I saw you with him."

Her arm goes limp and she sighs. "Aw, really?"

"Really. I hated seeing you with him." I blink hard. "Probably because he hogged all of your attention."

"I know," she says and motions to the photo of us. "Things have really changed since then."

I smile at the photograph. "It took me a long time to dig out of my funk. I can't really blame you guys for moving on."

Shauna's lips tighten. "Well, that's just dumb. We should've been there for you." She dabs the corner of her eye and wipes the goo on her jeans. "I should've been there for you. You're the one who lost your dad. Stop blaming yourself."

I rub my face hard. I'm tired of talking. Tired of discussing and reliving past events I can't change. "It was an accident. I have to leave it at that." I say the words aloud, but regret and guilt spread through me like an oil spill on a virgin coastline. It's ugly and toxic.

Shauna nods in agreement and repeats what I said. "It was an accident. Exactly." She straightens her homework papers. "I have to get going."

Pepper stretches on the floor and thumps her tail when Shauna stands and slips on her clogs. "Good seeing ya, Pepper," she says, stroking Pepper's head.

I step over the lazy mutt and check the clock. "I have to order pizza before I wake Mom. I'll walk you down."

I grab the phone and walk Shauna out onto the porch. Pepper squats next to the lily garden. I wonder if it's just my imagination or if the lilies really have grown a few inches today.

"Thanks for letting me come over," Shauna says. "Let's get together again soon."

Pepper follows Shauna to her car and tries to nudge her way into the driver's seat when Shauna opens the door.

"Take her. Please!" I kid. I snap my fingers. "Get over here, goof!" Gravel crunches under the wheels as Shauna backs up. Pepper plants her butt on my foot and whines.

"Don't cry, she'll be back." I wave as Shauna puts her car in drive.

"Hey." She sticks her head out of the window. "Let me know how things go with Trent."

I give her a thumbs-up. "Okay."

Pepper snatches a jagged piece of gravel and drops it at the screen door. "No. No more rocks," I tell her. She slinks into the kitchen and plops into her bed. "You can have pizza crust in a bit." I dial Dough Dough's

Pizza, and, as if Pepper understands me, she perks up her head and wags her tail.

With the delivery guy expected within thirty minutes, I go to wake Mom. The cold air coming from inside her room stops me in the doorway. I rub my arms and shiver as I go over to the air conditioner and click it to medium.

"Leave it on high," Mom says, her voice deep from sleep. She sweeps her fingers across the base of the lamp next to her. With a soft touch to its base, it illuminates the room. A smile spreads across her face.

I smile back, clicking the air to high and then mosey over to the lamp. I touch it over and over. "Off. On. Off. On."

Mom scoots to the edge of the bed and grabs my hand. I pull her up. She takes a step to test her balance. I watch her face for pain, since I know how she is. She tries so hard not to show it. "My cane," she says, and takes another two steps. Her left foot is slow to catch up, so she switches the cane to that side.

Over the years, Mom's made lots of adjustments to everyday functions. Walking, speaking, turning on lights. Back when she still saw Dr. Collins, he advised us to revamp our house with gadgets that were "MS friendly." Even though Mom hated that phrase, she liked the idea of saving strength in her hands. She replaced all the table lamps by ordering touch lamps, and I removed all the doorknobs on the first floor. She was so happy to be able to work the lever handles and not have to grip anymore.

We thought she could save her gripping strength for the steering wheel, but that didn't last long, either. Last fall, right before my first Behind the Wheel session, she had to turn in her license. She tried not to show how upset she was; when Jed offered to take me driving, she said she was crying happy tears.

But the thing I hate right now is that our last stinging session didn't help like it should have. Like it used to. Every slow, painful step Mom takes is just one step closer to her trying the record dose. Which she wants me to give to her.

Pepper and I follow close behind as she inches her way into the living room. I help her into the antique rocker and jump when Pepper barks. Mom holds on to Pepper while I pay for the pizza.

Spicy pepperoni and sausage aromas fill our living room. I sink into the battered sofa. Pepper sits bug-eyed between Mom and me. Her statuesque composure is interrupted only by an occasional shiver or slurp of her tongue. I divvy up the pizza and give us each a piece.

"I was starved!" I toss my crust to Pepper, who devours it before I have my second slice on my plate.

Mom catches a stream of sauce on her chin and stuffs her napkin into her palm. "Shauna couldn't stay?"

I shrug. "I didn't ask her to."

"Why not?" Mom asks. She leans forward and looks me in the eye.

I gulp my coke and spit an ice cube into my glass. "I don't know. I guess I need to feel her out before we do a pizza night."

Mom pats my knee. "You've been friends ... since kindergarten."

"But we haven't been close since Dad died. You know that." I wipe the bottom of my glass on my jeans. "Plus, she just broke up with her boyfriend so she'll probably find some rebound guy and I won't see her much anyway. Unless she needs a book." I take a big bite of crust and chew hard.

Mom looks at me sideways. "Do you want ... to be her friend?"

"I wasn't the one who stopped being friends." I pick a sausage off my pizza and pop it into my mouth. Pepper sighs and scoots closer to Mom.

Mom raises an eyebrow at me. "Lily."

"Okay. You're right. It was nice having her here today." I push my plate toward Pepper and fold my legs to the side. "It's just not the same."

"You have to move forward ... through change." Mom glances at the picture of Dad that hangs above the television. "Sometimes, change is ... for the best. Even if it's hard."

And there it is. Another hint that my life will change even more. She's trying to prepare me. Trying to make sure that I'm surrounded by friends and not left alone once she's gone. I'll give her that. "Friends are good," I say in my best impersonation of Jed.

Mom laughs. "Yes, they are."

I sigh and think about the old days with Shauna and Emily. Those images are quickly replaced by thoughts of seeing Trent in the morning. We've been riding partners before—first on tricycles, and then on ponies—so I'm glad for this second chance at friendship. I rub my sweaty palms on my knees and remind myself to breathe. I don't want to worry about what Emily is going to think. Let her think we're more than friends.

It's not an impossible scenario, but all I know right now is that it's nice to have my old friend back. For the rest of the night, while I clean the kitchen and help Mom to bed, and until my head hits the pillow, he's the one on my mind.

Seven

Early the next morning, warm drizzle swirls in the air. It clings to Ms. Spidey's web. "A horsefly today," I say, cupping the stunned insect in my palm. I mount Twilight, stand in the stirrups, and peer into the tightly spun hole leading to a crack in the lumber. "Come and get it."

As soon as she feels the vibration of the fly on the web, Ms. Spidey is out of her hiding place like a frenzied vampire. She goes in fighting and jabs her fangs into the meat a few times before retreating to safety. She pokes out of the hole one last time. "It's dead," I say.

Twilight's breath thickens in the mist as we reach Jed's grain silo. Trent is nowhere in sight. My hair is plastered against my face. I rake my fingers through the tangles after tying Twilight to a fence post. The drizzle grows into a steady, light rain. Dark clouds tumble and roll in the distance.

"Nice day for a ride," Trent shouts as he rounds the bend. A trickle of rain spills off his hat like a waterfall.

"Looks like the clouds are moving the other way." I point to the sky. "Should we wait it out?"

He motions to the overgrown pasture next to Jed's house. "Let's get them under the lean-to."

The lean-to houses a dozen swallow nests, and the birds swoop in close and warn us with their clicking.

"Man, I hate those birds." Trent ducks and bobs every time a bird rushes him.

"I think they're awesome. They eat like a thousand insects an hour." I watch one swallow as it flies high into the gray sky before dive-bombing straight toward me. I stand my ground as it comes inches away from my head and then zooms off.

Trent grabs my wrist and tows me away. "Let's go to the silo."

Bits of stone crumble around the door frame as Trent yanks it open and we get inside. My nostrils sting from a musty sour stench. "Leave the door open."

"You afraid of the dark?" Trent teases, forming his fingers into claws.

I step closer to the fresh, rainy air coming through the door. "No, just of the rotting stink."

Trent raises an arm and sniffs his armpit. "Oh, good. It's not me then." He steps closer to me.

My laughter echoes through the silo as I step away from the door. My gut flip-flops when he reaches toward me.

"You're freaked out in here," he says as he pulls a blade of grass out of my hair.

I lean against the cool stone and kick the ground. "Am not!"

Trent looks up toward the highest point of the tower and shouts, "Hello!" It echoes twice, making us laugh.

It's quiet for a few seconds until we hear someone outside clear their throat. "Having fun?" Emily says, her sarcastic voice booming into the silo. She glares at me from the doorway. "Is she your sloppy seconds, Trent?"

I glare back at her. "Hello to you, too."

Trent rushes her and grabs her by the shoulders, keeping her out in the rain. "What are you doing here?"

Her lemonade hair sticks to her face as dimples dance on her chin. "I got up early to come to your house to talk, but then I spotted your horses over there. The question is, what are *you* doing here?" She looks over his shoulder at me before I look away.

Trent releases his grip. "We were going to ride, but it started raining." He clears his throat and rubs his hands together. "But that's really none of your business now."

Emily scoffs and wipes her face. "A ride? Right. I'm not stupid, Trent."

I step next to Trent. "It's true. Rocky needs the exercise. That's all."

"You don't need to explain, Lily," Trent says.

Emily cocks her head. "Yeah, shut up, Lily."

A distant rumble of thunder makes the horses whinny.

Trent shakes his head and steps out into the drizzle toward her. "That's not what I meant, Emily. *I* don't have to explain either. I'm done with you telling me who I can hang out with."

She backs away, flinging her hair. "Fine then. Have your sloppy seconds."

I step out of the silo and see the clearing sky. "I'm sick of you treating me so shitty," I say. I swallow a lump in my throat. "We used to be friends. Go home, Emily. Sloppy Seconds and Trent are going riding now."

Trent bites a knuckle to stifle his laugh.

Emily stomps toward her car as Trent and I head to the lean-to. She honks as she peels away, making us both turn to look. Her arm sticks out of the window. Her middle finger waves in the air.

"Hey, she's calling us number one." Trent laughs and thrusts his own middle finger at her.

"She needs to make up her mind," I say, my hands on my hips. "I thought I was Sloppy Seconds."

Trent stops and raises his chin. "Are you?"

A little gallop in my chest makes me forget to breathe for a second. I flick my wrist and manage to say, "No, it was a joke." When he looks a bit deflated, I want to take it back and tell it him it wasn't a joke, but I'm not a hundred percent sure myself.

"Everything all right out there?" Jed yells from his porch.

Trent spins around at the sound of Jed shouting to us. We step through the overgrown grass toward the sidewalk. "Fine, Jed," I say.

His overalls are half snapped and his morning stubble is so thick it makes me think of chocolate jimmies. "I was just frying some eggs," he tells us. "Come in and join me?"

I look at the clearing sky and then at Twilight. Before I can say no thank you, Trent speaks for both of us.

"Eggs sound good. More filling than the frozen grapes I have in my saddle bag." He runs a few steps toward the horses and calls to me, "Go on in, I'll get the grapes."

I'm surprised at the condition of Jed's living room. It's so tidy, it appears the room is never used. A crocheted blanket is draped over the back of the sofa and the fireplace is clean of wood or ash. The yellow and pink floral cushions are tucked perfectly in place.

"It's so cheery in here," I say.

"Yes, the missus had a way with decorating." Jed pats a side chair and nods his head. "She redid this room right before she passed."

I swallow hard, realizing why the room is so neat and unused.

"It's a lot of house for one old man," Jed adds. He leads me to the kitchen, where the aroma of melting butter makes my stomach growl. "I mainly stay in here if I'm not sleeping." He switches off a small television propped on top of his microwave.

Trent is back, opening the side door and knocking at the same time. He wipes his boots and holds out the grapes. "They've thawed out, but they're still tasty."

"You like scrambled or fried?" Jed holds an egg up. "I like fried."

"Fried it is," I say quickly, and shoot a look at Trent.

He gets my drift and goes with the flow. "Fried for me, too."

Once the pan is sizzling, Jed pours a round of orange juice. "What was all the commotion out there by the silo?"

Trent sighs and lays his forehead on the table for a second. "Ex-girlfriend trouble," he mumbles when he comes up for air.

"The wrath of an ex can be soothed." Jed flips the eggs and winks at Trent. "Tell her she's too good for you. That she deserves better."

"Jed!" I balk at his suggestion. "Why should he lie and let her off easy?" Trent remains quiet. His gaze ping-pongs between me and Jed.

Jed sets plates in front of us and then smiles. "To let himself off easy, Lily. A spurned woman is a wicked force."

Trent laughs and mashes his eggs into bits. "You're a wise man."

I dip my toast into a yolk. "Fine, kill her with kindness even if she doesn't deserve it. You're only going to feed her ego."

Trent and Jed share a male bonding nod, so I give up and change the subject. "Any lookers for the house yet, Jed?"

"Some folks are coming by this afternoon." He checks the clock and takes his last bite of breakfast. "They have four little children."

Trent belches and excuses himself. "Why are you moving? Where're you going to?"

Jed passes a smile my way and takes our dishes to the sink.

"Well ... " I stammer, trying to find the right words. I rub my forehead and try to keep my eggs down as they tumble around in my gut. "Jed is going to be living with me and Mom."

Trent straightens his back and rests the heels of his boots on Jed's chair. "Jed! You and Sophia?"

I swat Trent's hand as Jed laughs. "Sophia and I are good friends, is all," he says. He buckles the fallen strap of his overalls and checks the clock again. "We were always like one big family when Lily's dad was alive." He nods in my direction and pauses. "You could say I need them as much as they need me and my help around the house."

Trent's face softens. "Oh, I see," he says, blinking at me.

No you don't! Don't look at me with that pity in your eyes.

"This stays between us. Okay?" I say to him.

"Sure. I guess." He fumbles with his napkin.

Jed comes to my rescue. "Until it's a done deal, with the house sold and all, we're not advertising it." He pushes Trent's feet off his chair, making him lurch forward.

"That's fine. I won't tell anyone." Trent stands and shakes Jed's hand. "Thanks for the eggs, man."

"Good luck with the house showing later," I say, giving Jed a little hug. His prickly stubble scrapes my temple.

"We'll talk tomorrow." He waves while Trent and I head to the lean-to.

Trent unties the horses in a hurry as I watch for incoming swallows. I wipe off Twilight's saddle, settle onto him, and lead the way to the field.

The warm sun penetrates my damp clothes, making me shiver for a second. The swallows swoop in the muggy air. Grasshoppers scatter. I pull Twilight back so Rocky can catch up. Trent has a big grin on his face as he meets my stride.

"I was enjoying the view from back there," he teases.

"Oh, knock it off." I feel my face flush at the thought of him checking out my ass. "You want to ride or what?"

"Sorry. I can't help it." He shrugs his shoulders, still flashing his I'm-so-charming grin. "There's something about a girl on a horse I find attractive."

I roll my eyes. "Sure. Even if it's Sloppy Seconds, huh?"

He breathes in deep through his nostrils and tilts his head. "I've always preferred leftovers."

I throw my head back and laugh. "Oh my God, you are so full of it." I bring Twilight to a halt and let Rocky get in front of me. "How do *you* like it? Can you feel my eyes glued to your butt?" I stick my neck out and stare at his backside.

He raises up from his saddle and wriggles. "Nice buns, huh?"

"Sit your butt down and ride," I say, shielding my eyes and laughing. Then I nudge Twilight and fly by him. I run Twilight toward the lake that separates Jed's land from Trent's.

The trail leads to the edge of the woods, where I hop off Twilight and take in the glistening water. Red-winged blackbirds take flight, leaving their cattail perches swaying in the breeze. Twilight heads to the shoreline and sucks up water. Trent walks out of the woods. He's all muddy on one side and leading Rocky by the reins.

"He threw me off!"

I can't help laughing. "Rocky, that was naughty."

Rocky and Twilight wade into the lake as Trent cleans his hat in the shallow water. He sets it on a large boulder and looks at his shirt. "This is trash now." He rolls up the hem of his T-shirt, revealing the band of his gray boxers and his inny belly button.

I feel my eyes widen, followed by a thump in my chest. As the shirt goes over his head, I catch myself staring. This place is already gorgeous, but he just made it breathtaking.

He pulls the shirt off completely and lets it dangle from his thumb.

I grab it. "Trash? I don't think so. It'll clean out." I crouch down, plunge it into the water, and scrub.

"I got a million of these shirts. It's no big deal," I hear him say behind me.

I huff as I turn to throw the shirt at him, and find him standing on a large boulder pouring water from his hat down his chest. The sun beats down on him. His skin glistens like a newly waxed car. He stops rubbing his abs when he catches me watching.

"Thanks," he says, reaching for the shirt.

I wad it up and throw it at him anyway. It hits him right in the face with a splat.

"Hey! What'd you do that for?" He peels the shirt off his head and laughs.

I squint at him. "Because you're a brat, that's why."

He takes long strides toward the water, digging his boots into the sand. "I'm a brat?" He fills his hat with water and rushes toward me.

I scramble to get up, but he's too quick. He pushes the hat onto my head, dousing me with cold water. "Who's a brat?"

Water drips down my shoulders to my chest and back as he lifts the hat off my head. "You're a spoiled brat for not caring about your muddy shirt," I quip. "And now you're going to get it." I pull off my left boot and fill it with water as he refills his hat.

Our weapons held high, we begin to circle each other. I wait for the perfect moment to splash him, but his green eyes never leave mine. He stalks me and reaches for my free arm. I thrust the water out of my boot. It ripples down his chest as he grabs my arm, pulling me up against him. His mouth is warm and sweet and his body slippery and cool.

He presses his lips harder onto mine. Every fiber in my body relaxes, and my hands instinctively find their way to the back of his neck. For a moment, we are all that exists in the world.

Then reality creeps in and I push away. "I'm sorry," I say, wiping my lips. "We shouldn't do this."

He smiles and nods. "But we did."

He steps closer, his hat still full of water. "You're the brat now." He threatens to dump the hat on my head before putting it on himself, letting water stream down his shoulders and bead away.

"Let's get these horses some exercise," I say, putting on my boot. I click my tongue for Twilight. He wades over to me and I hop onto him. "Follow the lake to your house?"

Trent stuffs his wet, sandy T-shirt into his bag and climbs onto Rocky. "You first," he teases.

"Hardy har har." I roll my eyes and lead the way. A frog dives into the lake and a blue heron takes flight. My shirt clings to me as I shake the ends of my hair.

"I'll get you a towel when we get to my house."

We follow the curve of the lake until we see Trent's house. I spot his dad's Cadillac in the parking circle.

"Maybe I should just head home, Trent. Mom's alone, and I should get back anyway."

"No, no, come on to the house," he says, then notices the car. "Don't worry about him. He'll be in his office."

I take a deep breath. "All right. But I'm going to stay outside." I click my tongue and head to the barn. "And remember not to say anything about Jed."

Trent swipes his finger across his chest. "Cross my heart."

We tie our horses to a post behind the barn. I don't tell Trent, but I'm glad I'm not in view of the house. "I'll take Rocky's saddle off," I offer. "Why don't you get some towels."

Before he leaves, he unpacks his T-shirt, some left-over grapes, a pack of crackers, and a hunk of cheese from his saddlebag. He smiles when he sees me watching. "In case we got hungry."

"Good idea," I say, even though I'm thinking, *that's sweet!* I watch him walk away toward the house. My pulse quickens. *It was more than sweet. It was romantic.*

I hang Rocky's tack and let the horses into the pasture. I use a glossy steel feed bucket as a mirror and comb my fingers through my hair.

Trent appears in the doorway, dry with brushed hair. He tosses me a towel and I begin squeezing my hair. "Got a comb?" I ask.

"Your hair looks good to me," he says, but reaches into his back pocket anyway.

I pick up the bucket again and see my big hair reflected in it, all tangles and puffy. "Good for the eighties, maybe," I say as I quickly run Trent's comb through it.

"You know, I didn't mean to embarrass you at the lake," Trent says.

I look around to be sure we're alone. I spot Max and other workers laying sod near the driveway. "I wasn't embarrassed. Just a little shocked."

He steps closer to me and I quickly give the comb back to him. Our fingers touch as he says, "I really like you, Lily."

I step back. It would be so easy to fall into him and admit how much I've missed him. I'd love to admit that I've liked him since we were little kids, but I can't let it go there. It's easier this way. I don't need to deal with the drama from Emily and the issue of Dr. Collins. I swallow hard, realizing that taking the easy way out really sucks.

For a second, I think about using Jed's line and telling him he's too good for me. Instead, I tell him what I really feel. "You're just on a rebound from breaking up with Emily, that's all."

Trent fingers his hair and sighs. "No, that's not true. I'm not rebounding or trying to make Emily jealous or anything like that. I've always liked you." He clears his throat. "I'm pretty sure she knew that, and that's why she didn't want me seeing you."

"That figures." I glance at the Cadillac and swallow hard. "Still, with the hard feelings between my mom and your dad, I don't think it'd be a good idea for us to be more than friends." Even though Mom doesn't mind, I do. Family comes first.

He bites his lip and kicks a pebble. "That sucks."

I laugh and huff at the same time.

"No, I didn't mean it like that!" He slaps his forehead. "That's my way of saying I'd like to be more than friends, but being friends will work, too."

"Friends and riding partners?"

"You bet," he says, and yanks a T-shirt hanging from his belt loop. "Dry shirt?" He holds it out for me. "Go ahead and change in the stall. I promise not to peek."

I slip into the stall and change quickly. I tie the bottom of his T-shirt into a knot around my waist. I exit the stall, strutting like a runway model. "For the summer collection, we see that men's T-shirts are all the rage."

He folds his arms across his chest and breathes in deep through his nose. "See? Right there. That's exactly what I like about you." His nostrils flare as his chest expands. "It looks fabulous."

I fold my wet shirt and whistle for Twilight. "I have to get home and check on Mom."

"Tell her I say hello."

We walk to the pasture fence and I hop on Twilight. Rocky heads to his stall. "He seems better already," Trent says.

"Sometimes, a little TLC is all they need." I smile and nudge Twilight.

Trent leans against the barn and jerks his head. "Keep the T-shirt. I've got a million of them."

I roll my eyes and snort. "You brat."

He grins wide. "See you tomorrow?"

"Not unless you're planning to help me clean." I raise my eyebrows. "That's how I always like to spend my Memorial Day."

He grimaces. "All work and no play makes Lily a dull girl." Then he smiles and adds, "We should change that."

I just laugh. "See you at school, Trent."

I take it easy on Twilight on the way back to the house. No galloping or running. I inhale the scent of my new shirt and sigh as we pass the silo. "Riding partners, Lily. That's all," I whisper.

Eight

Our gravel driveway is dotted with puddles of left-over rain. Dragonflies zoom about, taking sips of water before it evaporates in the midday heat. As I kick off my boots and toss them onto the welcome mat, Pepper spins on the kitchen floor and then bolts for her stuffed zebra. I catch a glimpse of Mom closing the blinds in the living room.

"Hey, Tiger," Mom says when I find her stretched out on the couch. "It's a hot one ... today."

The coffee table has some legal-looking papers and three stacks of files strewn across it. *House. Medical. Lily.*

"So how was your date?" she asks, lingering on the last word.

I shoot her a playful evil eye. "Stop it." I feel my face flush.

"You're blushing." She sits up and pats the cushion beside her. "Come on. Tell me why." Her eyes beg for a tiny bit of detail and I know I have to give in.

I flop onto the sofa and sigh. "He kissed me and it was nice and weird all at the same time."

Her face lights up like she's seeing me walk for the first time. "Oh, Lily!"

"Don't get too excited. I told him we're better off just friends."

Her shoulders slump a little. "I see," she says.

In a matter of seconds, I'd given her hope and a glimpse into my life, then dashed it all away without thinking. "For now," I add. "We're just friends for now."

"And friends are good." She winks at me, leans back into the cushions, and sighs deeply.

I lean forward and reach for my file but Mom sets her foot on it. "Not now, sweetie." She sits up and gathers the papers. "I need a nap." Her arms, shoulders, neck, and head wriggle as the papers slip into one another.

"Leave them, Mom," I say, rubbing her shoulder. Her tremor sends vibrations all the way up to my elbow. "I won't look through them. I promise."

She takes deep breath and lets her arms fall to her lap. "I'm sorry."

I wrap my arms around her. I hug firmly and absorb her quaking. "Don't be sorry, Mom. You've nothing to be sorry for."

We're wrapped together for almost ten minutes before her breathing becomes slow and steady and her body still.

"Let's get you to bed now," I whisper.

I hook my arm around her as she shuffles beside me to her room. Pepper tiptoes alongside with her ears down and the zebra dangling from her mouth.

"Can I get you some ice water, or tea?"

She melts onto the bed and closes her eyes instantly. "Crank the air."

I switch her air on full blast. It sputters as Mom lets out a moan. I swivel around to see her pushing Pepper away from her.

I snap my fingers and point to the door. Pepper jumps down and slinks out of the room.

Mom's propped up on an elbow. Her eyes are wide and flicking side to side. She moans again. "Get my waste basket."

I snatch the basket from beside her bed and hold it under her chin. She gags and squeezes her eyes shut. I wipe her forehead and hold her hair back while she vomits.

She pushes the basket away and rests on her side. "It's the heat."

I dab her face with a tissue. "Oh, Mom. Maybe I should stay in here with you."

"No." She covers her eyes. "I just need ... to be still."

I pull the liner out of the wastebasket and tie it. "Get some rest now."

The red light on our phone glows in the darkened living room. I pull the window shades up halfway, letting in some warmth along with the light, and hit *play*. There are two hang-up calls before I hear Shauna's voice.

"Hi, Lily. It's Shauna. Get your ass out of bed. Mom found a date and freed me from wedding duty. It's going to be stifling hot today. Wanna go swimming or catch a movie? Call me."

I'm tired from riding and worried about Mom, but the thought of a swim sure is tempting. Half of me wants to go, and the other half is saying stay until Mom gets up. I throw a load of towels in the washing machine. My swimsuit top dangles on the drying rope in the laundry room. It's crispy and still smells like the hay I hauled the last time I wore it. *Oh, who cares. It's only Shauna.* "Just go," I tell myself.

I punch her phone number fast. Her voice is all excited when she answers.

After we make our plans, I make a few sandwiches. I wrap one in foil for Mom, put it in the refrigerator, and toss the other two into my school cooler.

Mom's been sleeping almost an hour by the time Shauna pulls into the drive. I race to the door to be sure she doesn't ring the doorbell and make Pepper bark. Pepper pushes through my legs, nudges the screen door, and bolts to Shauna.

"Hey, Pooch!" Shauna slaps her thighs and crouches to greet her. "She's such a great dog, Lily. Should we bring her to Miller's Pond?"

Before I can answer, Shauna's getting Pepper all wound up. "Wanna go swimming? Wanna catch a stick? Oh, you're a good girl!"

I pick up a stray tennis ball and laugh as Pepper jumps into the back seat of Shauna's car. "Guess there's no saying no now. I'll get a towel for her and let my mom know I'm leaving."

When I peek into the room, Mom's breathing is deep and heavy. It won't be long before it's a good snore, I'm sure, so I leave her a note and place it on her water glass.

> Went to Miller's Pond with Shauna. Back
> at dark. Turkey sandwich in the fridge.
> XXOO Lily

I reach the screen door and suddenly have this urge to go crumple that note and stay home after all. I feel like telling Shauna I can't go. Then I spot her in the driver's seat, wearing some ridiculously huge sunglasses while

Pepper licks her cheek. I smile and click the door closed behind me.

Pepper sticks her head out as we cruise the back roads toward our old swimming spot. She sneezes and snuffles and aims her nose to the wind. Shauna flips through the radio stations and settles on a country tune. She belts it out, singing along to lyrics about a cheating man. She knows every single word.

I crack up laughing until she socks me on the shoulder and keeps on singing. I join in, trying to learn the words as I go. When the song ends, she clicks off the radio and turns onto the dirt road.

"You've got a good voice," I say. "It's funny that you know that song, because it sure doesn't seem to fit you."

Shauna rolls her eyes and throws the car into park under a large oak tree. "*Fit me?*"

I swallow and try to explain. "Well ... yeah. You're not very 'country.'" My feeble attempt only sticks my foot deeper into my mouth.

She strums her finger across the row of hoop earrings that hang from her right ear. "Don't *assume* that I'm a headbanger. I like all sorts of music." She grabs her stuff and hops out of the car, Pepper on her heels.

I try not to regret making plans with her as I gather my things and catch up with her. "I can't believe we used to ride our bikes all the way here," I say as I lay my towel down.

"Yeah. Those were fun times." Her tone is a bit cold now. She whips the tennis ball as far as she can into the lake and Pepper's on it before Shauna even sits down.

I pick at an acorn shell and take a breath. "Shauna, I didn't mean anything back there. It doesn't matter to me what kind of music you like."

She gives me a half smile and sighs. "I know. I'm just tired of people judging people on what they wear, what they listen to, what kind of car they drive. All that crap."

I hoot. "You don't have to explain that to *me*. I feel judged all the time. Or maybe it's pity. I'm always getting the sense that people judge me because I have one parent, live in the boonies, and wear hick clothes. Yadda yadda yadda. The fact that you know country music in spite of what people think is a good thing. It keeps you interesting. Keeps them guessing, you know?"

Shauna laughs and nods her head. "That's the name of the game. Keep them guessing."

I bite the inside of my lip and fling the acorn into the water. "Not much to guess about me now, is there? Most people think I'm up to my elbow in manure half the time, and they're right!" I laugh. "I have 'country girl' written all over me."

Shauna slaps her leg. "A country girl who doesn't know country and an ex-goth who's not a headbanger. Fine pair we are!"

"Yeah, who the heck are we, anyway?"

Shauna stretches and rolls onto her stomach. "I'm not sure, but I'm glad we're finding out."

I grin at that as Pepper approaches us with the tennis ball. She shakes, spraying us with cool muddy water. I jump up and rub my face and arms.

Shauna flies onto her feet and rips off her shirt, revealing a tiny, leopard-print bikini top. She pats herself dry and catches me checking out her suit. "It's my mom's. It's cool, isn't it?" She adjusts the small triangles of material, trying to keep herself from popping out, and then slides her jean shorts down. She kicks them onto her towel.

"It is," I say, trying to sound convincing. "I think you'd make the cover of Playboy in that one!" As soon as I spew those words, I fear Shauna will take it wrong again. I'm relieved when she doesn't.

She struts and purses her lips. "A cover girl who likes country!"

"Keep 'em guessing!" I say. I hop out of my shorts, exposing my long legs and yellow, boy-cut bikini bottoms. I peel off my T-shirt and suddenly feel twelve years old again. As if Shauna has grown and changed mentally and physically while I'm stuck in time somewhere. It feels a bit surreal to be hanging out with her. We were such good friends before Dad died, and here we are again. Only this time, it's Mom I'm losing. But there will be no blaming the world this time, and I'll try to be a better friend. I hope she does, too, because I don't want her to bail.

Shauna races Pepper to the water and dives under. I stand at the shoreline and test the water with my toes. Jed's words lap the surface of my brain. *It's not good to be alone so much.* I wade in fast, trying to keep up. Trying to catch up with Shauna and lost time.

We float on our backs and soak in Oregon's record-breaking May heat wave. The chorus of spring peepers is almost deafening as Shauna nudges my side.

"I said, 'How was your ride with Trent this morning?'"

The rays suddenly feel hotter and make my skin prickle. I splash my face and dip under. When I come up for air, I smooth my hair back and smile innocently. "It was fun."

Shauna cups her hand and splashes me. "Fun? That's it? I want details."

"Of course you do, Miss Million Questions." I giggle and push weeds out of my path as I wade toward shore.

Shauna scoops them up and winds them around her wrists. "Did he make a move on you?"

"We're just friends, Shauna." I wrap a towel around my head. "Riding partners."

She stretches the triangles of her teeny bikini to their absolute fullest and still can't cover up fully.

"That's not what I asked you. Did he make a move on you?"

I plop down onto my towel and Pepper lays her soggy head in my lap. "Oh, all right. Yes! He kissed me." I hurry through my words. "But I told him we're just friends. Riding partners."

She studies my face and squints. "Riding partners. Right." Her skeptical, lawyerlike tone makes me squirm. "I don't believe it for a second, Lily."

"Well, it's true. Trent and I go too far back as friends to be anything more." I sound convincing, even to myself. "I can't be more than friends."

Shauna opens her cooler and hands me a Coke. "Why? Because of Emily?" She takes a gulp of her own.

"Emily has nothing to do with this." I throw back my head and laugh. "If anything, I'd date Trent just to piss her off."

Shauna covers her mouth, nods her head, and leans forward, trying to keep Coke from spewing out her nose.

"Really," I say. "He told me she didn't want him asking for my help with Rocky and threatened to break up with him if he did. So he broke up with her."

Shauna snorts and can barely get her words out. "He broke up with her over his horse! I love it!" She slaps the ground. "But really, it was over *you*. He's always had a thing for you, and that's irritated the crap out of Emily." Her face beams as she says this. "It's a good thing she has Betsy as a sidekick now or she'd be all alone." She makes an exaggerated frown face and laughs again.

"Boo hoo," I add, pulling our lunch closer.

As the sun dips its bottom into the horizon, a neon path of orange rolls out before us. I dig into my cooler and toss Shauna a sandwich. A pang of guilt collides with my hunger. I think of Mom, eating her sandwich alone.

"You two would make a cute couple," Shauna says with her mouth full. "Too bad you don't like him." She watches me while she chews and then swallows. "Maybe I'll go after him."

My jaw drops. "I never said I didn't like him," I blurt. I bite my lip when she nods, all cocky. "You'll make a great lawyer," I tell her. "You just totally baited me."

"I don't have to be an attorney to see that you like him." She pushes my shoulder. "Right?"

"Shauna," I say, stroking Pepper's head, "our parents aren't super fond of each other. I think I started to pull away from Trent after his dad was so uncompassionate toward Mom and the bee stings. As much as Emily would like to think it was because she had some magical hold on him, there's more to it than that. I can't be more than friends with him even if I wanted to."

She sits up straight. "But you would if you could?"

I remain silent. Plead the Fifth. But the answer that pops into my head is *yes, I would be more than friends*. Right now, though, Mom comes first, and doing anything that would upset her is not on my To Do list. It's a small sacrifice to make.

"Oh, wow," she says, pulling her T-shirt on. "It's like *Romeo and Juliet*! Forbidden love!"

I roll my eyes. "Not exactly. Mom wouldn't forbid it. I just wouldn't be able to look at his dad knowing…" I pause and backtrack. "I just wouldn't be able to look at his dad. Period."

Shauna fiddles with her row of hoops and stares into the sunset. "You're deliberately holding back on me. I can tell. You're feeling me out to see if you can trust me."

I study the side of her face as she continues to watch the scenery. "I'm not sure I can even trust myself, Shauna."

She faces me. "What the heck is that supposed to mean?"

I shrug as we gather our stuff and pile into the car. Moths and insects attack the headlights as we drive the dirt road. Pepper stinks of algae and fish shit. She's in her glory as her ears ride the wind.

Finally, I take the plunge. I swear Shauna to secrecy and tell her my real-life version of *Romeo and Juliet*. That I do have a crush on Trent but can't get past the fact that his dad couldn't help Mom and then made her feel silly for trying the BVT. That I doubt Trent cares what his dad thinks, but still, it's his dad and I wouldn't want to come between them. And that I'm trying to be Trent's friend but I don't know if I can trust myself with him.

Shauna whistles. "Oh boy."

I tell her that even though I promised Mom I wouldn't look at the files, I peeked at the first page of the one with my name on it. I couldn't bring myself to look at the ones marked *House* and *Medical.* "I suck at keeping promises, too. Consider yourself warned."

"I would've done the same thing," she says. Then, in true Shauna fashion, she asks, "What'd it say?"

"It was her will, and it was all this legal mumbo jumbo stating everything would be left to me." A drip forms at my nostril and I sniff it in. I rummage through her glove compartment for a napkin. I answer Shauna's questions until my throat hurts.

She rubs my kneecap. "Don't cry."

"Leaving everything to me is quite ironic, actually." I exhale and slide myself against the door. "See, the thing is, Mom doesn't want to quit the way you think she does. She wants me to help her. If a high dose of stings doesn't work, she's done." I breathe in slowly. "Seeing the will made me sick to my stomach." I can't look at Shauna's face.

One hand reaches for her cross while the other tightens around the steering wheel until her knuckles turn white. "You'll be all alone? She really asked you?"

The answer squeezes out of my brain. "No, Jed is moving in for a while. Yes, she really asked me to let her die." Saying it all out loud has me shaking.

My head spins like a sideswiped car out of control. I find myself answering Shauna's questions methodically, without reservation. "No, Trent doesn't know any of this."

Her last question breaks a moment of silence. "Are you going to do it?"

My mind argues with itself. *No! What, are you crazy? That's like murder! Yes! Of course I'll help her. Why would I want her to continue to suffer? No! She's living whether she likes it or not. Yes! I'll do it whether I like it or not. Yes? No?*

We pull into my driveway and Pepper jumps through the back window before the car is fully stopped. I stare at a crack in the dashboard. "I haven't decided yet," I say. "But with my help or not, I'm afraid she's made up her mind."

I look at the house. Everything is pitch dark. A wave of panic rolls my insides when I realize the porch light isn't on. I scramble out of the car. *I should have stayed home with you, Mom. I'm sorry!*

Shauna leans on the passenger seat and looks up at me. "Damn, Lily. Are you sure she's in her right mind?"

A gasp of breath escapes me. "Right mind, wrong body," I say, slamming the car door. "My mom's the smartest and most realistic person I know." I stomp away, fuming and worried as I make a beeline for the darkened porch.

"Sorry!" Shauna shouts after me. "I didn't mean it like that."

The pounding of my heart drowns out the sound of Shauna's wheels crunching gravel as it rolls away. I step into the quiet kitchen. *Mom's still asleep?* I turn, ready to call out to Shauna, *Wait! Don't leave!*

But it's too late. I'm alone. Alone with questions pounding in my heart. *What if she's… what if Mom is already…*

Nine

I throw my things to the floor and fumble for the row of light switches. The porch bulb flicks on when I test it. My fingers tremble as I turn it off and touch the kitchen lamp. I rake my fingers through my damp hair and rush to the refrigerator. Mom's turkey sandwich is untouched.

Pepper sticks her face into the fridge and snuffles. I nudge her with my knee as I shut the door. "Get out of there, you stupid dog!" Hot tears trickle down my face. I fall to my knees and grab Pepper, pulling her toward me as she cowers. I plunge my face into her furry shoulder. "I'm sorry, sweetheart," I whisper. She laps up my tears and then follows me toward Mom's bedroom.

I flick on the chandelier in the dining room, casting some light into Mom's room. The hum of the air conditioner fills the silence. I focus on the heap under the sheet until my eyes adjust and I see my note perched on her water glass, right where I left it.

My chest tightens. My body becomes rigid. I suck in staggered breaths. "Mom?" I whisper. Her back is facing me. She's curled up on her side with her arm stretched out behind her. I clear my throat. "Mom?" I say a bit louder.

Pepper reacts with a thump-thump of her tail. She moves to Mom's bedside and sniffs. Her tail wags harder while she sniffs deeper and deeper, finally licking Mom's hand.

The sheets roll as Mom stirs. I burst into tears and rush the bed. Pepper whines and frantically licks. Mom stretches and yawns. She sits up abruptly and wipes my face. "What's wrong?" she says, oblivious to my fears.

"Wrong?" I say and pat the bed, giving the all clear to Pepper. She springs up in one leap and nuzzles next to Mom.

Mom traces my eyes with her thumbs. "Are you crying?"

I wipe my face, smooth my hair, and lie. "No. I was swimming." I flick on her reading lamp and grab her comb off the nightstand. "It's almost eight o'clock. You should eat. I made you a sandwich."

She takes my note off her glass and reads it. "You're a doll, Lily." She eases off the bed and wraps her summer robe around her before taking my elbow.

On our way to the kitchen, we shuffle through the living room. "What's all that?" I ask, directing my chin toward the stacks of files on the coffee table.

She sits at the kitchen table. I set her sandwich in front of her, along with a glass of iced tea. "Papers for the lawyer next week," she says.

I roll a napkin between my palms to soak up my sweat. I dab my forehead and let my breath out. I try not to let on that I peeked at the will. "Do I need to be there?"

She swallows and takes a sip of tea. "No. We're just signing papers." She sets the half-eaten sandwich down and pushes the plate away. "Papers for my ... living will."

I shake my head and plunk my chin onto my palm. "Living will?" Now I wish I'd dug into the files more. "That's a medical thing, right? Papers saying you don't want to be hooked up to tubes and machines to keep you alive?"

She doesn't speak a word. She just nods in agreement while she slips the turkey off her sandwich and offers it to Pepper.

My jaw stiffens. I know she's thinking about Dad. She has to be, because that's exactly what comes to my mind when I think of being hooked up to machines.

And it's just too much to think about. I shoot out of my chair so fast, it tips. I grab it before it hits the floor.

Mom leans back quickly. "Lily!"

"What?" I shout. "You're getting all your ducks lined up in a row and I don't have to like it, Mom." I point to the stacks on the coffee table. "It all looks so organized, but what about me?"

"You'll be taken care of." She nods at the files. "There's also a will."

"That's not what I mean!" My arms flail as I turn toward her. "You know how sad you were when Dad died? Well, that's going to be me. ME." I stand there, facing her. "That's going to be me, missing you." I pound the side of my fist on the table and hold back tears.

"I know," she whispers. "I'll miss you … too. It's breaking my heart."

I slide into my chair and look to the ceiling. "You're giving up! Well, I'm not. I want you to see some other doctor. Get help. What you want to do, what you've asked me to do"—I pause and catch my breath—"is selfish." I lower my head and look into her eyes.

"Lily," she says, taking a hold of my hand. "Dr. Collins is one of the best … neurologists in the country." Her bony hands squeeze tighter. "I wish I could stop what is happening … to me. I want to be here. Believe me." She blinks hard and clicks her tongue. "To see you date. Get married." She stops and takes a few deeps breaths. Her nostrils flair like she's holding back tears. "To see my grandchildren." He eyes become far away and she smiles, as if she sees my future.

"I'm sorry, Mom. I didn't mean to upset you." I bow my head. Tears drip onto my lap. I want to see the happy future she sees for me, but all I envision is being without her. Alone.

She clears her throat and lifts my chin. "Nothing can make me better. But, I can try ... to make it easier ... for you." The veins in her neck bulge. She holds up a finger to signal she's got more to say. "Jed and I are talking about ... guardianship ... for you."

It's all almost more than I can take in and I can't help showing it. I shake my head. "Guardianship." When I repeat it, it comes out like swear word. "Seems that'll help both of us, huh?"

She frowns at that and sighs.

I go to her side and hug her fragile frame. I'm filled with an intense desire to make sure she knows how I feel about her. *Her.* Not the MS or the guardianship or the living will. "You're the best mom and I love you so much." I take in the lilac scent of her. "I know being sick isn't your fault, and sometimes I wish it was me instead of you. If it was, I know you'd do everything you could to help me."

My throat tightens around the words I say next. "I've thought about your idea, and I'm scared, but we should try the sixteen stings." I breathe again. "Only to see if it helps you, though. That's all. I'm sorry if I'm being selfish." But the truth is, I'm not sorry. If clinging to a thread of hope and not letting her go is selfish, then bring it on.

"You're not selfish," she says, hugging me with all her might. "You're a good, strong daughter and I love you, too." She holds me an arms-length away and nods. "Tomorrow." Then she laughs, waving her hand close to her face. "But right now, you smell like fish."

I crack up laughing. Pepper prances toward us and nudges my side. She scrambles away to grab her zebra. Mom and I watch her shake it with violent pleasure before rolling onto her back. She balances it with her front paws as she gnaws on it.

"Goof," Mom says.

I see the simple joy in Mom's eyes as she watches Pepper. Her smile is tender as she takes in the moment. I suddenly realize how lucky I feel to have this time with her. It's my simple joy.

Mom stacks her dishes and inches herself to a stand. Her arms jerk when she holds the table to steady herself.

"Let me help you," I say, and step next to her. She grimaces, turning her face away from me while reaching for me. Her palm is cold and clammy. "I got ya," I tell her as she takes a small step.

"To the bathroom," she says.

In the time it takes for us to walk the length of the kitchen, I feel her strength increase a bit and her skin warm up.

I flick on the bathroom light. "You want some help in there?"

She shakes her head and forces a smile. "No, Tiger. I don't."

I close the door behind her and lean against the door frame. I hear her do her business and flush and I know she'd be mad and embarrassed that I'm listening. I hear her fumbling around and wonder if I should knock. Then the sounds of running water and teeth brushing make me feel better. The *tap tap* of her toothbrush against the sink has me sprinting away from the door over to Pepper, who's lying a few feet away.

She opens the door and looks perturbed to see me sitting on the floor next to Pep. "You're waiting for me?"

I can't lie. She knows darn well that I was. "Just making sure you're okay." I get up, stretch, and offer my hand to her.

Her face softens as she steps toward me and grasps my arm. She takes a deep breath. "I'll be fine on the couch."

I help her arrange a stack of pillows and push the coffee table closer when she motions for it. The papers and files are all within her reach now.

She reaches for the file with my name on it and pauses. "I'm almost done."

"Okay," I say after giving her a kiss on the cheek. "I'll leave you alone. I'm going to get ready for bed. Shout if you need me."

She nods and looks at the staircase leading to my room. I know she misses being able to use our second floor. She hasn't been in my room or her old bedroom for a few years. Moving out of the room she shared with Dad was so hard on her. But there wasn't any choice, after it became clear that going up and down stairs just wasn't safe anymore. Setting up her room in the den was Jed's idea. Good ol' Jed. I was so glad he talked her into it.

Pepper stands with a groan. She follows me up the first three stairs until I tell her no. "You stay with Mom." She turns back and when I hear her plop down, I continue to my room, hoping that she's smart enough to come for me if Mom needs something. The thought makes me sick to my stomach, so I prop my bedroom door open just a crack. Just in case Mom calls for me.

Ten

I wake to the cardinal's song and slap my alarm before it buzzes. I get a glimpse of my door. It's wide open and Pepper's sprawled out on my floor. A lump rises to my throat. "Dang it!" I say through my teeth. "You were supposed to stay downstairs, Pepper!" She lifts her head and looks at me for a second before slowly getting up.

"Some guard dog you are." I gallop down the stairs and stop at the landing. Mom's still on the couch. The files and papers are stacked together now and bound with a big rubber band. The floor lamp next to her is still on, casting a creamy glow onto her face. Her dark hair is messy and as I get closer, I see movement behind her lids. I let out a sigh and turn off the light before heading to my room to get dressed.

I pick out a red tank top with blue and white stars on it. I can still be festive even though I'll be spending Memorial Day catching bees instead of picnicking.

Back downstairs, I let Pepper out and wolf down a bowl of cereal while Mom sleeps peacefully. As soon as I let Pepper in, she pounces through the kitchen and skids up next to Mom. She laps and licks her face before I can shoo her away.

Mom stirs and wipes her cheek. She squints at me. "Morning."

"Sorry, Mom," I whisper. "I wanted you to sleep."

She motions for me to come to her, so I do. I take both of her hands and help her to her feet. She heads to the bathroom. "I'll get you some coffee," I say.

"And toast, please," she says, closing the door.

The toaster's innards glow a dark honey yellow. I glance over my shoulder and look outside, where my beekeeper veil hangs in the shed. *Please, let sixteen stings work. Please.*

Mom comes in, wiping her face on a towel. She's changed into her tattered cotton robe. Its pockets bulge with tissue and the neckline is stained from hair dye. It smells of baby powder. I love that robe.

I set her buttered toast and coffee in front of her and grab a yogurt for myself. We eat without talking, but we both know today's a big day. Pepper watches my every spoon-to-mouth movement until I finally let her lick the container.

Mom finishes her coffee and hands me the empty cup. "Fill 'er up and take it to my room." She stands and shuffles across the kitchen floor.

I fill the cup, catch up to her, and help her into bed.

"Get the bees now ... Tiger Lily." She smiles as she says my nickname.

I kiss her forehead. "I'll get the ice and numb you down first."

She nods and unties her robe, baring her frail legs and exposing the greenish-tinged bruises from her last treatment.

Pepper's nails tap across the kitchen floor when she hears me crack the ice trays. She rears, over and over, waiting for a cube. I toss one in the air for her. She trots off with her head held high and crunches the cold treat in seconds. I step over her, and over the small melting puddle she's created, and pause at the stereo. I switch on Mom's jazz station and let the music soothe me for a second. I take a deep breath and let it out slowly. "Please let this work."

I help her get comfortable on her bed and place the ice packs on her arms and legs. "We'll sting your neck and back last, today. Let these sit and I'll be right back with the bees."

Pepper follows me out the door and to the shed. My hands tremble as I don my beekeeper garb. Our two hives are set up near the sugar maple, just a few yards away from the horse pasture where Twilight grazes. As I approach the hives and unscrew the lid on the bee jar, I see Twilight sauntering over to the split rail fence that separates us.

"Hi ya, sweetlips," I say in response to his neigh.

I pull off the access plug and quickly set the jar in place. When I tap the backside of the hive, a few guard bees fly into the jar. They buzz and ricochet off the glass bottom. Within a few minutes, I have about twenty-five bees sealed in the jar. For a split second, I think about setting them all free and calling the whole thing off.

Pepper pants in the shade behind me.

"Move, Pep. Or I'll step on you."

She snaps at a few loose bees and gets up with a moan.

Twilight nods his head repeatedly and swishes his tail. He neighs and sputters until I finally reach over the fence for him.

His wheat-colored mane is soft, yet coarse. I scratch behind his jaw, just below his ears, where he likes it. "Gimme a kiss, Twilight."

He raises his nose and wriggles his fleshy lips, showing his teeth. I turn my head and present my cheek to him. "That's my sweetlips," I say, stroking his nose. "I'll come back after dinner and we'll ride."

Pepper slides under the fence rail and trots alongside Twilight. Twilight tries to spook her with a quick side step, but Pepper dodges out of the way. They romp and tease while I shove my supplies away in the shed.

"Come, Pepper," I call from the doorway. "Let's go get Mama."

As soon as I get into Mom's room, I spray the bees with a mist of water. I don't even bother marking X's on the sting spots anymore. Old bruises are my guide now.

The first set of eight stings is the easiest. Two in each leg, in the tender points of the thigh and shin. Two in each arm just below the shoulder and elbow. We take a break so I can mist the remaining bees. They've regained their strength and seem to be pissed. I aim the bottle and give them a good dousing.

"Here's your water, Mom," I say, wiping her forehead.

"You should be … a nurse."

"No. I don't think so." I turn away, clenching my teeth. *I do this because I love you, not because I enjoy it.* I put ice packs on her hands and feet.

She blinks and stares at the bee jar.

"Besides," I say, "I want to be a veterinarian just like you."

Once the bees are calm again, I pluck one out with my tweezers. "Hold still." I hold her hand firmly to control her tremor. I aim for what's left of the fatty pad between her thumb and index finger. It's tricky with her being so thin now.

The bee goes limp as I pull it away from its stinger, left throbbing in Mom's flesh. I put pressure on the skin around the stinger to ease the discomfort while the venom sac empties into her.

Mom's face tightens. She squeezes her eyes shut.

I look away and squeeze my eyes shut, too. She hardly ever shows her discomfort. She's always been good at hiding her pain. I wince for her and scrape the stinger from her flesh. I kiss the swollen spot. "Are you sure you want to do the rest?"

"Seven more . . . to go."

After I prick her other hand and both feet, a sinking feeling rumbles in my gut. "This is it, Mom. We've done twelve stings. You've never had more than that at one time." I search her eyes for any hint of concern. "Are you still sure we should do this?"

"Just four more, Lily. I have to know."

"But what if sixteen stings really is too much? You know you could go into shock. Or worse." My chest suddenly feels very heavy. The last time it felt this way, I was saying good-bye to Dad. "You're not trying to end your pain for good today, are you?" I bite my lip to keep it from trembling.

She looks to the ceiling and tilts her head.

"Mom! Are you?" My heart jumps into my throat. I suddenly feel frantic.

"No," she finally says.

I squint at her. "I agreed to do this to see if it helps you. Nothing else!"

"Get the EpiPen," she says. "Just in case."

A sigh of relief comes over me and I can breathe again. I turn her onto her stomach and place two ice packs at the base of her neck and two on her lower back, just above her butt. While they numb her, I get the EpiPen from the cabinet by the window.

When I turn back and see her lying there, face down, her frail body speckled with old and new bruises, I thank God. *Thank you for letting me have her a while longer.* Then I curse him. *Why won't you ease her pain? Why are you making me do it?*

I tuck the EpiPen into the hammer pocket of my jeans before checking the bees.

Mom takes the ice pack off of her neck. "Ready." She motions to my pocket and grins. "Fits perfect."

I glance at the EpiPen and feel a rush of panic. "This expires next month. You'll have to call Dr. Collins for a refill."

She rolls her eyes and curls her lip.

"I'll call him for you, then. Once a year, that's all you have to put up with him for."

She nods and grunts an okay. I pinch her neck to check for numbness. She doesn't react, so I give her the thirteenth sting.

After I scrape the stinger from her neck, I watch her breathing closely. "You all right?" I wipe beads of sweat off my nose and fan myself.

"Ah uh."

I dip my hand into the jar. The tweezers clink against the glass. Bee fourteen gives in without a struggle. "Ready?"

She gasps before I can sting her lower back.

"What?" I turn her onto her side and brush her hair away from her face. "Mom?"

She winces. "It's okay."

"No. No, it's not. You're wheezing and your eyes are getting puffy." I hold the tweezered bee above my head so I can snatch the hand mirror from her dresser and hold it in front of her. "See? You're having a reaction to the venom. We have to inject the antidote now."

She pushes the mirror away and motions to the bee. "One more ... sting."

My molars gnash as my whole body begins to tremble. "You said you weren't trying to end your life today." My legs wobble when I step away from her and hold the squirming bee in front of me. I toss the mirror onto her bed and feel for the EpiPen in my pocket. "I never said I'd let you die. Especially not like this."

She extends her hand to me. "Lily ... I didn't plan this." Her chest sinks as she gasps. A tear flows from the corner of her eye and melts into the sheets. "One more bee ... Please."

"I can't." I brush the bee against my forearm until it jabs me. The venom burns as it travels up my arm and down into my fingers. The injection site throbs instantly, like a hundred mosquitoes bites in the same spot. I suck in a breath and drop the tweezers to the floor.

Mom purses her lips and closes her eyes. Her head sinks deeper into her pillow. "Oh, Lily."

I pull the cap off of the antidote and step close to her. "I can't let you go this way." I thrust the injection into the side of her thigh and sob. I crumble to my knees and rest my forehead on her leg. "I'm sorry."

"Shhhh ... don't cry," Mom whispers.

The EpiPen rolls from my grip before I stand. I massage her thigh and place an ice pack on it. I'm numb. Our test has failed. Thirteen stings are more than her body can handle.

She turns her face away and wipes her eyes. "Too much and not enough."

"It should be enough to help the pain," I say, but when she turns to look at me, I realize that's not what she means. "You'll feel better, Mom." I try not to sound angry and grab the mirror again. "Look, your color is back in your lips. Just let the venom do its trick."

She scans her reflection and sticks out her tongue. "Yes, ma'am," she says, pushing the mirror away.

I roll her onto her back and push an ice pack under her neck. "You scared me." I put my hand on her chest. "I've read about anaphylactic shock from an allergic reaction. It's horrible. You know that. Your tongue would've swelled up like a tennis ball and suffocated you. You can't expect me to stand by and be a part of something like that."

She nods and closes her eyes. "I'm sorry."

Her eyelids are still puffy and I know it'll be hours before they're back to normal. I sit on the edge of her bed for a few minutes. I watch her and listen to her breathing. It's not raspy, and when she begins to take deep, clear breaths through her nose, I breathe a sigh of relief. "The antidote is working already. You rest while I clean this up."

I know the treatment takes a lot out of her. It takes a lot out of me, too, and I need some fresh air. I gather the bee jar and EpiPen and quietly leave her room.

I toss the EpiPen on the counter by the phone and take the bees outside. I stand on the porch and watch Pepper dig up a rock and roll on it. Over and over. I unscrew the lid of the bee jar and listen to their angry buzzing. "I hate you," I whisper.

I step down into the lily garden and set the jar on its side, hopping quickly back up onto the porch. It takes a few seconds of the bees bouncing against the lid before it falls away from the jar. When it does, they fly away free and head back toward their hive.

My hands start shaking and I have to sit. I hold my knees tight and rock myself on the porch stair. "I did the right thing, didn't I?"

Pepper stops mid-roll and looks at me.

"Yes, I did," I say, and leave Pepper to her rock love. I run in to check on Mom. She's zonked out. I pull a cool sheet up to her chest and slip out of the room.

I check my To Do list and start cleaning by rifling through a mound of laundry and throwing in a load. The washer chugs away, filling the house with a clean, soapy scent. I sweep the bathroom and kitchen and am pushing the dirt pile out the door when I spot Trent's truck coming up the driveway.

I hop back into the kitchen and wipe my sweaty face on my T-shirt, rubbing my teeth with my finger. I think about hiding until Pepper barks and I hear Trent slam his truck door. "Hellooo? I saw you sweeping, Lily. I'm here to help."

I smooth my hair, grab the broom, and open the door.

"Are you hiding from me?" he asks, looking at the pile of dirt on the porch.

I step over it, walk to the edge the porch, and lie. "No. I had to change laundry loads. I'm really busy, and my mom's sleeping."

He steps onto the bottom stair. We're eye to eye and I can't help looking at his mouth.

"I was only kidding around yesterday about you coming over to help me clean." I step back and sweep the dirt pile under the railing, into the garden below.

He steps up again and rests against the railing, blocking my way. He leans in close to me. "I thought I'd stop by and say hi."

His breath in my hair gives me goose bumps. I move aside. "Hi," I say, and tap the broom's bristles on the porch. "I really have to go check on my mom. Thanks for stopping by, though."

He nods and shoves his hands into his pockets, then jumps off the porch and lands next to Pepper. "Tell your mom I say hello." He pats Pepper on the head and starts toward his truck.

"Trent," I call, making him stop and turn around. "Don't stop stopping by, okay?"

He smiles wide and bows. "Until tomorrow, then."

I finish sweeping, change laundry loads, and empty the dishwasher. By the time I check on Mom again, she's reaching for her lamp and looking a little better. "Who was here?" she asks.

"Trent stopped over for a minute," I tell her. "He says hello to you."

She grabs onto my forearm and pulls herself up. "That's nice." She points to the living room. I settle her on the sofa and give her the remote. She clicks through the TV stations while I run a bath for her.

"Do you want to watch a movie tonight?" I yell over the rushing water. "Or play some cards?" I head back to the living room. "Mom?"

She looks away from some TV game show. "Pot pies and a movie would be nice." She reaches for me and I get her up and into the bathroom. "I can take it from here," she says and shoos me away.

"Just hold onto the bar when you get in." I feel my forehead wrinkle. "Please."

The door shuts and I spend the next thirty minutes sitting quietly on the floor in the hallway, listening and making sure she's okay. I have to. If not for her, then for my own peace of mind.

Eleven

The next morning, I tiptoe into the living room, where she's still sleeping on the sofa. She'd lasted about halfway through our movie before zonking out again, so I tucked her in and let her sleep there.

She stirs when I grab my backpack from the rocker. She pulls herself up, sits in a stupor, and looks around, trying to figure out where she's at.

"Good morning," I whisper. "Sorry I woke you."

"It's okay." She looks at me and smiles. Her left eye is droopy and bright licorice-red. "I need to get up."

I sweep my hair over one shoulder and zip up my gray sweatshirt. "I have to get to the bus. You want some juice before I go?"

She stands and gives me a hug. "I can get it. You go." She reaches for the arm of the couch, misses, and almost falls to the floor.

I leap toward her and catch her by the shoulders. "Whoa!"

She nudges me back. "I'm just sleepy." She rubs her eyes and blinks. When she looks at me, she blinks again. "Get my eye drops."

After I go to the bathroom cabinet and help her with the eye drops, I lead her to her bedroom where she just about walks into the door frame.

"This isn't funny, Mom. You're not seeing right." I help her into the lounge chair by the window. "Please let me stay home and go to the lawyer's with you."

"No. You can't miss school." She shakes her head. "Jed will be here soon." She puckers up, pats her lips with her fingers, and blows me a kiss.

"Stay here until he gets here," I say. I kiss her and head out of the house. Even though I'm worried sick, I tell myself she'll be okay for the short time she'll be alone. *Please let her be okay.* I jump from the porch, careful not to land on any lilies. They've grown at least five inches this week and are up to my knees. As I sprint by them, I notice one plant has a bright white bud. I smile, knowing Mom will be so proud. Her newest addition to her lily collection is doing well. I want to run back to tell her that the White Lace survived the winter and is budding, but I don't. I make it to the bus stop just as Jed pulls up and gives the horn a quick beep.

"Morning, Lily," he says. He's a bit too cheery for me in the morning.

"Morning," I say back, scanning the seats. I spot Trent's crew in the back as usual, but no Trent this time. I slide into the seat next to the door and watch Jed shift gears.

His lips form a thin line as he shakes his head slowly and swallows. "Toughie's not nursing. And her eyes look puffy."

I sink lower into my seat. "And?" I tap my foot against the chrome bar. I don't mean to be callous, but seriously, the last thing I want to talk about right now is Toughie.

He nods and switches gears. He looks over his shoulder at me and whispers, "There'll be a substitute driver this afternoon. I'll be with your Mom, but you can go see Toughie without me being home."

I sit up straight. "So, I'm now at your beck and call since you'll be living with us?" I snort. "And getting free vet care?"

"I didn't mean any such thing, Lily." He shoots me a quick glance before eyeing up the road again.

Over and over, I twirl a strand of hair around my finger and then back again as I think about Jed becoming my legal guardian. The reality of me without Mom shakes my insides. The taste of sour cereal invades my mouth. I swallow hard.

"Why are you doing this, Jed?" I say as the bus pulls in front of the school.

Wrinkles appear on his forehead. He looks confused.

I stand and lean in close to him. "If you weren't agreeing to all this, Mom might not be giving up so easily. No one ever asked me if I even wanted a guardian."

He covers his heart as the bus comes to a full stop. Kids peel themselves out of their seats. "You're like the granddaughter I never had, Lily. I'm helping your mom because she's my friend and I think your dad would want me to." He pulls a lever and the doors open.

Kids push by me and I want to push back. "How about helping me by butting the hell out?" I cut into the line and am out the door, into the school, and at my locker before my body finally stops shaking.

Shauna appears from around the corner and plants herself right in front of me. "Hey. I'm an ass and so sorry for sounding rude the other night." She holds her hand up when I try to speak. "I shouldn't have asked if your mom's mind is right. I don't blame you for being pissed at me."

I grab her hand and flick it away. "Shauna, I'm not *pissed* at you. I know you well enough to know you don't think before you speak." Her eyes flutter when I say this, and I continue. "You said nothing that hasn't crossed my mind, but you have to understand … " I pause and whisper, "I thought I was walking into the house to find my mom dead."

Shauna's eyes grow wide and peer past me. I grimace when I see Emily and Betsy within earshot, leaning into one another as they come closer. I slam my locker and only take two steps before Emily calls my name.

Shauna elbows me. "Ignore her!" she says through gritted teeth.

"Hey, I'm talking to you!" Emily shouts, and several kids in the hall look at me.

I stop and turn without a word.

Emily hugs her books to her chest and glares at me. "Stop trying to steal Trent from me, Lily."

I snort and roll my eyes. "I can't steal what's not yours, Emily." I glance at the clock above her and shift my backpack. "You need to get over yourself. He doesn't want you, and I don't want him."

Betsy steps closer and says, "That's not what we heard. We heard you wanted him pretty bad at the lake." She cocks her head and gives me a fake grin. "Isn't that right, Shauna?"

I bite the inside of my cheek and turn slowly toward Shauna. Heat spreads from my neck to my face. Before I can say a word to her, Shauna is in Betsy's face. "Shut up, you skag! We all know Trent's liked Lily all this time. Don't deny it."

All it takes is for Betsy to shove Shauna, and instantly Shauna's on top of Betsy, yanking her hair and shouting, "Don't. Ever. Touch. Me. Again."

Teachers and students surround us as the first-hour bell rings through the halls. Some kid yells, "End of round one, boxers to their corners!" Other kids laugh. Shauna's arms and fists are a blur. Betsy tries to push her away.

Principal Riley zooms in and yanks Shauna off Betsy, holding her arms at her sides. Betsy touches her bottom lip and starts crying when she sees blood on her fingers.

Mr. Riley pokes the air and shouts, "You, you, and you, get to my office now!" He leads the way as Emily, Betsy, and I follow him. He tugs Shauna by the wrist and scans the crowd. "The rest of you get to class."

"I'm bleeding," Betsy says between sobs. "She busted my lip."

Emily rakes her fingers through her hair and smoothes her blouse. "See what you've done?" she whispers to me.

Shauna and I are directed to the detention room while Mr. Riley talks to the other two in his office. Shauna rubs her knuckles and sighs.

"So how long did you wait before exposing my little kiss with Trent?" I fold my arms across my chest. She won't look at me, so I lean across the table and push her upper arm until she looks me in the eye. "Did ya get on the phone as soon as you got home, or what?"

She looks away. "No!"

"Well, what then?" I fight back tears and tip back in my chair. "And I hope you didn't spill any of my *other* secrets."

At that, Shauna looks at me again. "About your Mom? No, I swear." She stands and paces and fiddles with her earrings. "Betsy called me last night and asked if I wanted a ride to school. She said that Emily misses us and the four of us should hang out."

Part of me wants to believe that Emily really does miss us, but I don't get my hopes up. I slap my forehead. "Oh, Shauna, they baited you. Emily doesn't miss us. They just wanted the scoop on Trent."

"I know that now!" Shauna plops back into her chair. "I was stupid to ride with them. They acted all nice and then when I saw the look on Emily's face in the hall, I knew they'd used me. I'm so stupid."

I study her face and can see how terrible she feels. Like a puppy that just got busted for pooping in the living room. "Yeah, well, for a stupid girl, you throw a mean punch."

Shauna shoots a look of relief at me and starts crying. "I really fell for it, Lily. I wanted to believe it—that Emily missed us, ya know?" She wipes her nose on her knee and lets out a sob-laugh. "I guess you're not the only one who knows I don't think before I speak, huh?"

"Yeah, they had you pegged as their informant." I reach across the table and pat her snot-free knee. "Don't worry about it. All this crap over a guy isn't worth it."

Principal Riley swings the detention-room door open and swoops into the room. His quick gestures are nerve-wracking even when all is well, but now that we're in trouble, his manic movements are intensified. He plants his hands onto his hips and shakes his head. A police officer steps in and Shauna lets out a little gasp.

The officer nods at Shauna and clears his throat. "I'm Officer Vick. Let's get you something for those knuckles and take a statement."

I see the fear in her eyes as he reaches for her arm. "It's okay, Shauna," I say, and stand. The ten o'clock bell rings through the halls. "Can I go with her?" I ask when it's quiet again.

Just as the words leave my mouth, the guidance counselor, Miss Andre, appears in the doorway. She motions to Mr. Riley. They share a few whispers as Shauna and I exchange a few looks. I smile and give her a nod. She puts her wrists together and grimaces.

"Officer Vick, is Shauna being arrested?" I ask, even though I know I shouldn't.

Mr. Riley shoots me a glare. "That's not your concern right now, Lily."

Miss Andre smiles at Shauna, then swivels on her heels to face the principal.

"From what I understand," she says, "the information is given on a need-to-know basis, and since Lily was involved in the incident, she has the right to know."

Officer Vick leads Shauna around the table by her elbow. "You'll be ticketed for disorderly conduct and suspended for three days. It's the zero-tolerance policy."

Shauna's face relaxes until Mr. Riley reveals his fangs and hisses, "But if Betsy presses charges, the actions will go further."

"I need you to come with me, Lily," Miss Andre says.

"She didn't do anything!" Shauna bursts, making the officer tighten his grasp on her.

"Don't worry about it, Shauna," I say as we're led into separate areas of the main office. Shauna disappears behind Principal Riley's door. My nose and eyes begin to sting. I swallow hard and push back tears.

"It's hard to be strong, isn't it?" Miss Andre says when we enter her office. "No need for that in here. Let it out, Lily." She plucks a tissue from a flowery box on her desk and hands it to me.

I crumple it into a ball. "Am I in trouble?"

She moves her phone and half sits on the corner of her desk. She motions me to sit, too. "No, you're not in trouble."

I continue to stand. "Then I should get to class. I have a report due before eleven and don't want it to be late." I shove the tissue in my pocket. "I still have half an hour."

Miss Andre plucks another tissue and wrinkles her face. "Lily, we just got word that your mother was taken to the hospital about an hour ago."

"What!" I shout. A burn spreads from the center of my chest to every inch of my body. "No, no, no. She's at some lawyer's office. You're wrong." I should've never left the house. Why didn't I stay home today!

Miss Andre squeezes my shoulder. "I'll drive you to the hospital."

Her words bounce off me. "Mom wouldn't go to a hospital. There has to be a mistake." I glare at her and wait for her to agree, but she doesn't. She looks into my eyes and speaks very slowly, as if I'm dense.

"She was taken by ambulance, and I need to get you there."

I go through the motions of signing out in the office and following Miss Andrea to her car. My mind races with visions of Mom lying motionless in a hospital bed or arguing frantically with doctors. Between visions, I silently curse the traffic and keep an eye on Miss Andre's speed. "Turn here," I tell her. "It's a shortcut."

She looks confused but makes the turn anyway.

"I remember taking this street way back when Mom saw doctors," I explain. "My dad and I would pick her up after her appointments." I suddenly feel like Shauna, speaking before I think and talking too much.

Miss Andre nods. "I've read your case file, Lily. You've missed a lot of school, but you seem to keep up your grades. Good for you." She gives me a sideways glance and smiles. "I know you've been through a lot."

Do you now? I think sarcastically, wondering what my case file all says about me. I remain quiet, remembering Miss Andre's words to Principal Riley: *Information is given on a need-to-know basis.* I figure she needed to know because of all my absences. We'd gotten a letter from the school warning us about them and reminding us about laws and crap.

We pull under the hospital canopy where a valet parking guy takes over the car. He's already whisked it away by the time I realize Miss Andre is walking next to me, ushering me through the Emergency Room doors. My brain goes into overdrive. I can't get a good breath. Hospital staff and patients all seem to look the other way when my eyes meet theirs. And then I spot Jed.

Twelve

*M*iss Andre and I hurry past rows of beds, all separated by white curtains. Jed has his back to us and I can tell his arms are crossed. When he turns and sees us coming, his expression transforms from stricken to relief. He stretches out his arms and folds them around me.

"She's okay," he whispers into my hair.

I burst into sobs and bury my face in his suit coat. "What happened?"

He hugs me tight and rocks before holding me away. He stoops to get eye level with me. "She lost her footing and fell down a couple of stairs at the lawyer's office."

I glance at Miss Andre and sense her relief. She smiles at me and reaches her hand toward Jed. "I'm Jennifer Andre, the Guidance Counselor at Parkfield."

"Yes, I recognize you." Jed gives her hand a little shake. "I'm Jed Abrams. I drive for the school. Thank you for bringing Lily."

Miss Andre looks puzzled, so I explain that Jed is an old friend of the family. "You don't have to stay," I tell her. "I have to see Mom now, and Jed can take me home."

She pats my shoulder and nods. "I'll tell the attendance office about your absence, and please keep me posted on how your mother is doing. If you need anything, let me know."

The sincerity in her voice is sweet and unsettling, too. A flash of her studying my school file makes me wince. "Thank you, Miss Andre, I will." I watch her walk away.

"She seems like a nice woman," Jed says.

I ignore the comment and grab his arm. "Where's Mom?" The few minutes that have passed feels like an hour and I can't wait one more second to see her.

Jed motions to a curtained-off area and grabs my hand. "Lily. Before we go in there, I have to warn you that she's pretty banged up."

I close my eyes and try not to cry. A vision of Dad with a tube in his nose flashes in the darkness. I blink it away and feel every muscle in my body tense. Jed rubs my arm and tells me to breathe. I can't.

I enter the little cubicle and stifle my gasp. Mom's left eye is a slit, buried in swollen flesh the color of a ripe plum. Her left hand is bandaged and dried blood surrounds her fingernails.

"Oh, Mom," I whisper, and sit at her bedside. I kiss her right hand, hold it to my cheek, and close my eyes. I look up when I feel her squeeze my fingers.

She smiles and clears her throat. "You should see . . . the other guy."

Jed cracks up and nudges me. "That mom of yours, she's something else."

I rub her hand and laugh.

Our moment of silliness is cut short when Dr. Collins throws the white curtain aside and marches in. I shoot out of my chair and give Mom a wide-eyed look. She nods. "It's okay, Lily. It's just routine . . . hospital stuff."

Dr. Collins looks past Jed and me when he acknowledges us. "Lily. Jed. I need a few minutes with Sophia." His jaw barely moves when he speaks. He's stiff as a robot and has the bedside manner of a zombie.

"I'm staying," I say, planting my butt back in my chair.

Jed cracks his knuckles and looks at the floor. His casual defiance is a nice touch, but the cracking—and the way it makes Dr. Collins nervous—makes me smile.

A little redhead in a pink nurse's uniform pops in and hands Dr. Collins a clipboard. He flips through Mom's chart and clicks his pen over and over.

"I want to go home," Mom says. She reaches for me and pulls herself up to sit.

Dr. Collins touches her face lightly and shines a light into her eyes. "The deteriorated vision in your left eye is probably the cause of your fall. There's no sign of a concussion, Sophia, but any blow to the head that was hard enough to knock you out could be serious. I'd like to observe you through the night."

I lurch forward. "Knocked out? You didn't tell me she was knocked out."

Jed shakes his head and glares at Dr. Collins. "I was just about to."

Mom waves her good hand. "It doesn't matter. I'm fine." She inches her legs to the side of the bed and pushes the sheet away. As soon as her feet hit the floor, her knees buckle. Jed catches her in one swift move. He sets her down and gently guides her legs under the covers. I help tuck her in and feel the muscle spasms in her legs vibrating the entire mattress.

"Sophia, stay in bed," Dr. Collins says. "You'll feel better after a night of rest." He writes a note in her chart and hands it to Nurse Redhead. She gives me a half smile and disappears around the curtain.

"I've ordered an IV of..." Dr. Collins begins, but Mom cuts him off.

"No. No drugs."

The tension in the room squeezes my heart as Jed squeezes my hand.

Dr. Collins nods. "Okay, Sophia, no medications. Just an IV of fluids to help you get strong enough to go home. How's that?"

"Tomorrow," Mom says. "Home tomorrow." Her puffy eye twitches as the other one flutters. She's asleep before Dr. Collins finishes his notes.

"May I have a word with you?" he asks Jed and me, sliding his gold pen into his jacket pocket. As he holds the curtain for us, I can only think of one word for him: *asshole*.

He leads us to the nurse's station, where he hands Nurse Redhead the chart and mumbles a few words to her. A few steps away, we enter a tiny room and Dr. Collins closes the door behind us. Jed and I sit side by side on a stiff little sofa and the doc leans against the wall.

"I want to run some tests on Sophia but I need your help convincing her," he says.

"No way," I blurt, at the exact same time that Jed asks, "What kind of tests?"

Dr. Collins ignores me and directs his answer to Jed. "Blood work, brain scan, and a spinal tap."

"She'll never allow it," I say. The room seems to get smaller as I notice Jed nodding at the Good Doctor. He wipes his palms on his dress pants. "What's the purpose of these tests?" he asks.

"It's obvious that Sophia's MS has progressed very rapidly," Dr. Collins says. He pinches the bridge of his nose and avoids eye contact with me. "These tests will allow us to design a treatment plan for her."

At that I stand up and step toward Dr. Collins. "Treatment plan?" I feel the veins in my neck pumping. "She had all those tests and tried your treatment plan years ago. What makes you think it's going to work now?" He begins to answer but I cut him off. "You just want to keep treating her because it makes you feel better. Your plan did more harm than good."

The little room sways, and I step back to sit down. It suddenly hits me that the harsh words that just spewed from my lips sound as if they were meant for me.

Jed wraps an arm around me.

"Do no harm," Dr. Collins says. "I took that oath, the Hippocratic Oath, and strive to do what I can to help my patients. It's obvious the bee venom therapy isn't working. She needs to move on, away from the homeopathic remedies." He says those last two words like they're poison on his tongue.

Jed scoots to the edge of his seat. "Look, this isn't a debate. Using herbs and bee stings is Sophia's choice. Your drugs didn't help her before, and I know she won't use them again."

Even though my mind knows this, hearing Jed say it out loud makes my heart shudder. It seems that Dr. Collins senses my emotion, because his eyes pierce mine when he asks, "Doesn't your mom use traditional medicine at her vet clinic? On the animals she treats?" His lips curl into a smirk.

"We're not talking about an animal here, doctor." Jed stands and takes my hand. "Let's go, Lily."

My head swims with anger. "I know you think homeopathic medicine is quackery, and actually, we use both at the clinic."

Dr. Collins shakes his head. "This is about quality of care. Have you considered talking to her about going to an assisted living center?"

I blink hard. "A nursing home?" I stare at him, waiting for him to say it again. "You think I shouldn't be taking care of her? Is that it?"

He nods and buttons his coat. "Caretaking is a big responsibility, especially for a child. It might be of interest to Social Services."

"Is that a threat?" I sneer at him. If Mom hadn't taught me better, I'd spit.

Jed steps between us. "I'm in charge of her care now."

Jed's words shock me. I yank away from his grip. "I should report you," I snap at Dr. Collins. "Mom took an oath too, and one thing we never, ever do is let an animal suffer. We take good care of our patients and always consider their quality of life, too. Maybe you should try that."

Dr. Collins shifts his stiff posture. "I don't want Sophia to suffer."

I let out my breath and steady my chin. "Neither do I." My shoulder brushes against his white coat when I leave them behind in the tiny room. I'm tempted to just break Mom out of here. She wouldn't be in this place if I'd let her go when she asked me to. One merciful lethal dose of venom was her request. I'm sure no one would have questioned it. But I couldn't do it. I wouldn't.

The antiseptic-laced air stings my nostrils as I take a deep breath. The bright white hallway closes in on me. I hold onto the wall and I hurry to her room.

Thirteen

By the time I enter Mom's cubicle, Nurse Redhead is changing soggy bandages. Mom looks peaceful as she dozes. She doesn't even stir when fresh gauze and tape are pressed into place.

Jed comes in just as Nurse Redhead says, "We've decided it's best to move her to a regular room for the night." She cocks her head and puckers her lips to one side. "What are all these bruises from?" Her tone sounds more like a suspicious detective than a nurse. She sweeps her hand over Mom's body as if she's showing us something new.

"BVT," I say, testing her. I walk over to the corner where the IV contraption awaits. I scan the label to check its contents.

"That's saline," the nurse says. "I'm just waiting for the orders before I hook it up. It'll make her feel stronger."

I suddenly feel like she's testing me, now. Jed raises his brows and excuses himself to the hallway toilet.

"Does it work?" Nurse Redhead asks, as soon as Jed is gone. "The bee venom therapy? Does it work?" She rubs her wrist and gives me a genuine smile for once.

My smile back at her isn't as true, and I hesitate to answer. *Sure, it works if you can handle multiple stings until your body becomes immune to it. Give it four years.*

"Listen, whatever you tell me is strictly confidential. No charting of our talks. I'll leave that to Collins."

When she says "Collins," it's obvious she's not his biggest fan. I scan her nametag and offer a handshake. "Thanks for taking care of my mom, Gretchen." I'm about to tell her a bit about BVT when Collins and another doctor stroll in. Gretchen gets all flustered and scoots by me.

"Lily," Dr. Collins begins, "this is Dr. Brudmann."

He shakes my hand and nods. I'm silent. What am I supposed to say? *Nice to meet you?* No. *I wish I never had to lay eyes on you?* Yes. I just return a nod and stay quiet.

"In light of our discussion," Dr. Collins says, all robotlike, "your mother's care will be handled by Dr. Brudmann." He makes eye contact with me for a split second before staring over my shoulder. "I'll be acting as the advising physician from here on out."

I'm dumbfounded. I look to each of the doctors and then to Gretchen. She's got that half-smile on again and nods to me.

"From here on out? What does that mean?" My voice is louder than I intend, and Mom stirs behind us. "After suggesting all those tests, you're giving her to someone else?"

"Call me Dr. Mark," Dr. Brudmann says, flashing a smile. A gleaming white, genuine smile. I notice that he's wearing jeans and a Nike shirt under his white coat. "Dr. Collins and I agree this is in the best interest of your mother. There are some underlying issues here we need to address."

The physician-speak is getting on my nerves, but Dr. Brudmann—aka Dr. Mark—has a nice manner about him. I cut him some slack and grin just as Jed walks in.

"This must be Dr. Mark," Jed says, smoothing his tie before extending his rough farmer hand. "Nice to meet you," he says and I just about fall over. *NICE TO MEET YOU?* All the formalities are making me sick. Focus on my mom. Now.

Dr. Mark releases Jed's grip. "We've actually met once. Just briefly."

Jed knows this doctor? I squint at him, and as if there's a question mark floating over my head, he says,

"He's an old buddy of your father's, Lily. I heard he transferred here, so I asked for him." Jed wraps an arm around me and shakes me with pride. "Lily here is like my granddaughter."

We're interrupted when a pair of orderlies bustle in. "The room upstairs is ready, Dr. Mark." They hustle past us, unlocking the wheels on Mom's bed and wheeling her out the door.

"Lily," Mom calls. He voice is breathy. She reaches out. "Lily."

I grab the orderly's sleeve. "Wait!" I rush to Mom's side and lean in close. "I'll stay with you."

The room goes quiet when Mom lifts a shaky hand. She strokes my face and hair. "Feed Twilight," she says softly.

I shake my head. "I'll get Shauna to do it. I want to stay."

"I want to sleep. You go." Her eyes flutter and she's out cold again.

I kiss the hollow of her cheek and watch her roll down the corridor.

Dr. Collins leaves without a word and follows behind Mom's bed. Gretchen tosses bandages into the trash and says, "You should get some rest, too. She'll have more energy tonight after the IV is in place. Come back then."

Dr. Mark agrees and suggests we meet with him later. "It'll give me a chance to go over her records and plan a course of action."

There we go again with the physician-speak: *course of action*. I don't have the strength to tell him there won't be any course of action, but Jed does. "Mark, we'll talk about Sophia's wishes when we return." Their final handshake feels like slow motion to me. It blurs in my head as *Sophia's wishes* echoes in my heart.

I lean against Jed as we walk outside. I'm thankful for him—this slender farmer of a man who suddenly seems so take-charge strong. "Jed, I'm so sorry I bit your head off on the bus earlier."

He stops and lifts my chin. "Sweet, Lily. I would never hold that against you. No need to apologize."

When I hug him around his waist, tears come without warning. "Thank you for butting in, Jed," I whisper.

He rocks me and then holds me away, wiping my tears with his knuckles. "Looks like you've got company," he says when he looks up.

"Shauna!" I shout, watching her bound toward us. "What are you doing here?"

She squirts a stream of water into her mouth and offers me the bottle before rambling, "I was freaking out in Principal Riley's office, defending you and telling him not to suspend you too, and he told me you weren't in trouble, but he wouldn't tell me where you went with Miss Andre."

Jed interrupts us by jangling his car keys and leading the way toward the parking lot. As Shauna and I follow him, I tell her about Mom's fall. She gives me a play-by-play of her ordeal and how she's been kicked out of school for three days.

Then she smiles, all smug, and shrugs. "It was worth it. While my mom was signing the suspension papers in the office, I saw that Miss Andre was signed out below your name, and it said *hospital* in the reason column."

I huff and climb into the front seat. "So much for confidentiality."

Shauna's face drains of any expression. She puffs out her cheeks.

"What?" I say, trying to make eye contact with her as we climb in the truck.

"I saw Trent on my way out of school and told him what happened and where you were. He was worried. Confidentiality never even dawned on me," she adds in a rush.

"It's fine, Shauna," I say. I think about Trent getting close to me on the porch yesterday. One minute I'm thinking about Trent, and the next minute I'm thinking about Mom. My thoughts have collided and suddenly both of them are on my mind. Trent's worried about me. I'm worried about Mom. I press my hands against my stomach.

We drive in silence for most of the ride home. When we reach the stop sign on Half Mile Road, Jed's truck lurches forward and the butterflies in my stomach take flight as I remember something.

"Jed!" I almost yell. "What happened with the papers this morning? Did you get to sign them before Mom fell?" A rush of guilt for asking such a thing comes over me. It collides with a sudden understanding of why setting up guardianship was so important to Mom. And to Jed. I know now he's only been trying to do what's best for me, for us, and make good on his promise to Dad. I turn toward him and study his furrowed brow.

He stares at the road and nods before glancing over at me. "I'll be your legal guardian, Lily." He blots his nose with his sleeve. "It's all taken care of." He pats the stack of files between us.

Shauna reaches over from the back seat and pats my shoulder.

I cover my mouth and rock as my mind ping-pongs with emotion. "Shit!" The guilt I feel for being relieved nauseates me. I pummel the dashboard and stomp my feet in a fit. "Shit!" Part of me is pissed at Mom for setting up a future for me without her. But another part is growing without my consent—a part that gets it and is grateful. But I'll never give in to full acceptance.

Jed pulls into our driveway and throws the truck into park. He grabs my fists and holds them. "It's okay, Lily," he shouts.

Shauna jumps out of the truck and appears at my side. Tears stream down her face.

"It's not okay," I say, crumpling against Jed. The sobs pour out of me uncontrollably. "I shouldn't be thinking about what's going to happen to me now. How can I be so selfish?" I sigh in exhaustion and the tension in my body releases.

Jed lets go of my hands and hugs me. "You're the least selfish person I know, young lady. And your mom wanted to make sure you're taken care of."

I push away and study Jed's face. "So no one will take me away from here? Ever?"

"That's right," he says, stepping out of the truck. "This is your home and that will never change." He loads his arms with Mom's files and heads toward the house.

Shauna takes my elbow and I drag myself out of the seat. The second I look at her, I feel my lip start quivering again. I burst into a laugh-cry. "I've never seen you so quiet."

"I don't know what to say," she mumbles, kicking some gravel. "But I'm glad you'll be staying here. Your mom did the right thing."

I gaze across the meadow when Twilight whinnies. "Yes," I whisper. "She did."

Pepper can hardly contain her excitement when we all walk into the house together. She runs circles around us, licking our hands with each pass, and I think of how nice it must be to have a dog's brain and be so oblivious to the reason why Mom isn't here for her to greet. Shauna ushers Pepper outside for a long-overdue squat.

"Are you hungry?" Jed asks as he peels off his suit coat and tosses his clip-on tie into the garbage. "How 'bout soup?"

I reach in for the tie but Jed stops me. "I have no use for that anymore. It served its purpose." He fills the coffeepot and smiles. "I hate ties."

I chuckle. "Soup sounds fine. I'll be back in a bit." I hurry out the door. The whir of the can opener makes me look back. Jed's figure is a blur behind the screen. He's dumping chicken-noodle soup into a pot. He rubs his neck and sighs in unison with me.

It's Mom I long to see standing in his place.

Pepper jumps up the stairs and lands at my feet. She nudges her ball at my thigh and growls playfully. Shauna holds a tennis ball in each hand and smiles.

"How's your hand?" I ask her, hurling the ball toward the stable. Pepper bolts for it and I motion for Shauna to come with me.

"A little raw," she says. "It hurts when I bend it." She winces as she flexes her fingers. "My mom wasn't too upset about the fight today. She totally understood." Then her face drops and she rolls her lips in.

I can tell she feels weird talking about her mom. "It's okay to talk about your mom," I tell her. I open Twilight's stall and whistle for him. "It doesn't bother me."

"Okay." She picks at the door frame. "I feel bad that your mom is so sick."

I duck my head under Ms. Spidey's web as Twilight brushes past me. "Just help me with this feed, okay?"

Twilight snuffles the back of my head. I turn and wrap my arms around him. "You're a good boy," I say into his neck. "We'll ride tomorrow, I prom … " I pause, stopping myself from making any promises. "I'll see you in the morning."

Shauna strokes Twilight's head and offers him a carrot. "Would you mind if I crashed here tonight?" she asks as we head back to the house.

"Well, I'm going back to the hospital in a while." I stop at the lily garden and touch the White Lace lily. "But if you want to hang out here, that's fine."

Shauna grins and nods. "That's gorgeous!" she says, and stoops closer to the bud. "Look at it shimmer!"

"Mom will be proud." The aroma of chicken soup swirls in the air, and I suddenly feel so hungry I'm woozy.

Shauna puts her arm around me. "Maybe you should bring it to her after we eat."

I think about that as we shuffle into the kitchen and see the nice table Jed has set for us. "No, she needs to see it in her garden," I finally say, reaching for the basket of crackers. "Jed, this all looks so nice. Thank you."

"Of course," he says. "Trent called."

I almost spurt iced tea. "He did?"

"He's on his way over." Jed winks my way, palms his bowl, and drinks down the soup. "I'm going to run home, check the animals, and see how Toughie's doing. You girls clean up and I'll be back to drive you to the hospital."

Shauna salutes. "Yes, sir."

Jed's only gone ten minutes when Trent shows up. Shauna elbows me in the ribs when he walks right into the house.

"Hey, bruiser," he says to Shauna. "Your cat fight is the talk of the school."

Shauna hisses and laughs. "I was defending Lily, not you. So, don't let it go to your melon-head." She starts spraying the dishes

I snort. "Too late for that."

Trent stands between us and glances sideways at me. "Emily called and said she wants to talk to you. She asked for you to call her."

Shauna shakes her head, behind Trent. "Screw her."

"I can't deal with her right now," I say. "If she wants to talk, she knows how to find me." I toss a dishtowel onto the counter.

Trent takes my hand and holds it between us. "How's your mom?"

He glances at Shauna, who says, "She knows I told you."

The worried look on their faces makes my stomach drop. I step back, trying not to cry. I can't get a word out.

Trent closes the gap between us and holds my hand a little tighter. "My dad told me, too. He knows you're my friend and thought I should know." He lifts my chin and looks over my face. "Are you okay?"

My insides crumble. I can't hold it in. "I'm scared. I just want her to come home." I fall into him. When the clinking in the sink stops, I know Shauna's watching us. I bury my face in Trent's T-shirt. When he wraps his arms around me, the room goes quiet except for my sobs and the galloping rhythm of our heartbeats.

And then the phone rings.

Fourteen

I hold my breath after saying hello.

Jed's voice pipes in. "Lily, Toughie is in a bad way. I need you to bring medicine over here now."

"I'll be right there," I say. Shauna and Trent wear matching looks of dread. "I need you to take me to Jed's," I tell Trent. "It's the calf. She must be having another seizure."

Shauna unfolds her arms and stretches her neck. "I'm coming too."

I dash into the clinic and race around, grabbing vials and syringes and tossing them into Mom's medicine bag. The tangy aroma of its leather makes me think of her and how she let me play pretend with it when I was little. Only when the bag was empty could I stuff it with my Breyer horses and play veterinarian.

I stopped playing pretend with it shortly after witnessing Mom use it to put an animal down. I was eleven and Dad, Mom, and I were heading to town when we came upon an injured deer in the middle of the road. Its legs were crippled beneath its body. Mom grabbed her bag and jumped out of the truck. Dad was telling her to leave it alone, but she continued to approach it slowly. It swayed its head as its eyes bulged in fear. Mom flicked the side of a syringe and reached for the deer's leg. I covered my eyes until Dad told it me it was safe to look, and that Mom had sent the deer to Heaven.

I cried myself to sleep that night as Dad stroked my hairline and forehead. Every so often, his fingertips would sweep lightly across my lids, making them heavy, and bringing on the dream.

To this day, the images of that dream remain vivid. It was Heaven, and we were all there. Me, Mom, Dad, and all the animals I'd ever seen come to the clinic. Dogs, cats, rabbits, horses. And then there was the deer, the lone wild animal Mom couldn't let suffer. He was running and kicking in a field.

The vision of the deer vanishes as I sling the bag over my shoulder and head to Trent's truck. I climb in without a word, set the bag between my feet, and wish it were full of toy stallions.

After the short, somber ride, we enter the barn and find Jed practically lying on top of Toughie. Seizures ripple through the calf as Jed calls out, "Do something for this poor thing!"

I lead Trent and Shauna to Willow's stall. "Take her out of here."

Shauna's voice quakes. "Will she buck?"

Trent pats Shauna's back and winks at me. "Let me get her." He steps into the stall and ties the cow's strap. "Come on, big girl," he whispers as he guides her out.

Jed rolls off of Toughie when I kneel next to them. He's still in his dress clothes, his shirt drenched with what I'm sure is a combination of Toughie's sweat and his sweat. The calf's coarse auburn hair is matted, and it glistens with every heave of her belly. Her eyes flutter while her tongue laps the air.

"Jed," I say, taking his hand. "The Diazepam isn't helping anymore."

His eyes lock with mine as he sits upright. He looks from me to Toughie and back again before his eyes start to water. "What else can we do?" He strokes Toughie's head in a rapid motion. "What about BVT? Would that help?"

Shauna and Trent return and sit across from us. Toughie gasps and Shauna covers her face.

"No, Jed. I'm so sorry." I wrap an arm around him and whisper, "I know you love her, but I think it's time to let her go."

Jed wipes his nose with his sleeve and nods. "You're right. She doesn't deserve this agony. I want you to end her suffering."

"Can you do that?" Trent asks me. "I mean, don't you have to have your mom do it?"

I ignore Trent, unzip the medicine bag, and find the vial of barbiturate. "This will put her to sleep. Legally, Mom should be the one to give it to her, but I'll do it if you want me to."

In the middle of our circle, Toughie bellows and her limbs stiffen. She begins panting and each of us touch her gently, trying to soothe her. We're all quiet for a minute while she settles.

"I don't want you to get in any trouble," Jed says. "Show me how to do it and I will."

I fill a syringe with the barbiturate and tap the side to release any air bubbles. "How can I get in trouble for doing the right thing?" I give him a gentle smile and add, "I'm not afraid of trouble. Besides, who's going to tell?"

Jed glances at Trent and Shauna and sighs. He scoots closer to Toughie, coddles her head, and kisses her. "You go to Mrs. Abrams now, and rest."

Shauna sniffles and says a little prayer. "God bless Toughie. Let her rest in peace."

Trent clears his throat when I feel for a pulse in Toughie's front leg. I insert the needle under her skin, inject the fluid slowly, and extract the needle. In the few seconds I take to put it back into the bag, Toughie's body goes from stiff to completely relaxed and limp.

"She's gone," I say, checking her pulse. I rub her side and press my lips together.

Jed lifts his head off of Toughie's. Tears drip from his chin. He grabs me and hugs me hard. "Thank you, Lily," he whispers. "Your mom will be proud of you."

At the moment he says that, Willow lets out a long, sorrowful moo outside. It echoes through the valley and sinks my heart. Her baby is gone, and somehow she senses it. She's left to roam the pastures alone now.

Shauna gets to her knees and pokes me. "We've got company," she whispers.

A figure in the doorway moves toward us. "I thought that was your truck," Dr. Collins says. He comes into the light and stops short. "What happened here?" His voice sounds shocked.

His concern takes me by surprise. I can't find words.

Trent stands and comes to my side. "Jed found his calf dead and we came over to help him ... "

Dr. Collins steps closer to Toughie. Mom's medicine bag is at his feet.

Jed takes the bag, stuffs it under his arm, and says, "I have to call the veterinary hospital. They'll send someone to pick her up tomorrow." He walks a few paces and turns back toward us. "We'll leave to see Sophia in ten minutes."

Shauna and I follow Trent as he leads his dad toward the door. "What are you doing here, Dad?" Trent asks.

"My shift was over and I wanted to touch base with Lily and Jed." He looks at me before continuing. "I called and left a message on your machine, but when I saw Trent's truck, I thought it would be okay to stop."

For Trent's sake, I'm extra civil to Dr. Collins. "It's okay." And even though I'm afraid to know, I ask, "What's the message?"

"That even though your mom is now under Dr. Mark's care, I'll be available if you wish to contact me." He clears his throat and remains expressionless. "Or if you want me there tonight, when you discuss your mom's care with Dr. Mark."

I stagger back and Shauna grips my elbow. I regain my footing and pull my arm from Shauna's hold. "Why? So you can *advise* Dr. Mark to put her in a nursing home?" Flecks of spit fly.

Dr. Collins flinches but doesn't respond.

"That's exactly what she doesn't want to happen," I say, stepping forward. "Jed is in charge if anything happens to Mom, and"—I take a deep breath—"he'll be my legal guardian. So there'll be no need to contact Social Services, either." I feel like I'm wearing armor. I stand soldier-straight and grin.

Trent's eyes widen. He sidesteps away from his dad. "You want Sophia to go to a nursing home?" He squints and shakes his head. "And what's this about Social Services?"

Dr. Collins stands firm and raises his chin. "There are plenty of fine *assisted living facilities* available, and I simply made that recommendation. Regarding Social Services, it's hospital policy for me to alert that department to *any* concerns I may have for a child. As far as my concern for your well-being, that has been strictly confidential." He glances at Trent. "No matter how much I respect my patients and their families, my duties as a physician always come first. I take my oath very seriously and up until now, I've never compromised it."

His words swirl in my head as I look over at where Toughie lies. I blink hard as Shauna strokes my arm. "Up until now?" I ask.

He folds his arms across his chest and takes a deep breath. "The limitations your mom set for her care has made my job as a multiple sclerosis specialist very difficult. For me, it's about sustaining life at all costs. We've been at odds for years, but I've come to understand that for her, it's about quality of life. I respect that and it's why I assigned Dr. Mark to her. Sometimes providing the best care means having another expert step in. Dr. Mark specializes in palliative care." He holds out his hand to me.

Trent's eyebrows shoot up as he looks at his dad's hand. His chest rises and sinks again as his eyes meet mine. My knees feel like they might buckle.

"I understand what that means," I say. "He'll make sure she's comfortable." Sadness fills me as I shake Dr. Collins' hand. He's finally looking out for Mom. Then confusion rattles every inch of me. I want to shout, *What about my quality of life? Don't give up! Just sustain her life at all...* But then a vision of Mom in pain stops my mind from finishing the thought.

Willow bellows from the pasture again. I glance over at Toughie and blink hard.

Dr. Collins follows my gaze. "I'm sorry about the calf," he says.

"Me too," I say as we all leave the barn. "She's at peace now."

Jed is pulling his truck up. "Ready?"

Trent opens the truck door for me. "Want me and Shauna to follow?"

Dr. Collins clears his throat. "Regular visiting hours are over. They'll only let Lily and Jed in."

I shift in my seat. "We'll be fine," I say to Trent and Shauna. "We'll meet you back at the house later."

Jed leads the caravan of vehicles off of his property. As we head toward the hospital, I tell Jed about Dr. Collins' change of heart. When we pass my house, I use the side mirror to watch Trent's truck turn into the driveway. I'm surprised to see that Dr. Collins' Cadillac is still behind us.

I swivel around in my seat just to be sure. It's him all right. "If he was going home, he should've turned back there," I say to Jed. "He said his shift was over."

Jed adjusts his rearview mirror. "Looks like he's following us."

Fifteen

Dr. Collins is nowhere in sight when we park and head into the hospital. I pace at the front desk while Jed asks for Mom's room number. The tap-tapping of our shoes breaks the silence in the halls until we stop at the elevator.

Our reflections appear when the doors come together and close us in. My stomach dives when the elevator lurches and chugs us upward. I study the distorted reflection of Jed's flannel shirt. "How did you find Dr. Mark?"

Jed watches the numbers blink toward our destination. "I recognized his name from the staff list and asked for him. I knew he hadn't seen your mom since"—he pauses and focuses on me—"since your dad passed."

The elevator stops with a thud. I suddenly remember meeting Dr. Mark at Dad's funeral. In the long line of motorcycles, he was the only rider wearing a suit.

The elevator doors close behind us and I smile when I spot Dr. Mark up the hall. He's talking with Gretchen as she holds a purse in one hand and tray of food in the other.

Dr. Mark and Gretchen nod in unison when we approach them. "My shift is over but I'll be here in the morning," Gretchen says. She points her chin at Mom's room. "She's been resting."

Just then, Dr. Collins comes around the corner and stands next to Dr. Mark.

"I thought your shift ended," I say to him.

He nods and looks at Dr. Mark. "I've asked to shadow Dr. Mark to get a better understanding of his practice." He tugs the hem of his jacket. "You don't mind, do you?"

I shake my head. "It's fine."

Dr. Mark stoops to get eye level with me. "Before you go in..." he says in a slow, hushed tone.

I grab Jed's hand and stand tall, preparing myself for what he has to tell us. "What? What is it?"

"We couldn't put Sophia on the IV," Dr. Mark says. "Fluids are building up and it seems her kidneys aren't functioning properly."

"She won't allow us to run tests to confirm that," Dr. Collins adds. "But all the symptoms are there. Puffy skin and her lack of voiding are signs."

A rush comes over me and I rub my head. "Her face was puffy after the last stings." A flash of her lying in her bed before I stuck her with the EpiPen makes me wince. I'd made her look at herself in the mirror. "I thought it was a reaction to the BVT."

Jed squeezes my fingers. "Don't you beat yourself up about it. You couldn't have known."

Dr. Collins clears his throat. "Jed, we understand you've been assigned to authorize Sophia's medical treatment when the time comes that she is unable to."

Dr. Mark interrupts. "Or deny treatment."

Dr. Collins ignores him and continues. "As the advising physician, I have to inform you that dialysis is an option. We can insert a catheter to help her void."

Jed looks at the floor. "That means help her pee?"

I answer without using doctorly terms. "Yes, Jed, a catheter will release her pee." I hold back from shouting. "And dialysis means she'd be hooked up to machines."

Jed's face turns white. "Forever?"

A voice booms over the speaker and pages Dr. Mark. He checks his beeper and sighs. "Yes, Jed, forever. Sophia's form of multiple sclerosis continues to cause damage to her organs even during her good days.

Even with dialysis, I'm afraid she'll only have about six months."

I melt into Jed. "What about without treatment?" I swallow and cover my mouth.

"A very short time, Lily," Dr. Mark says. "Possibly days."

I burst into tears and hold my stomach. "Days?" I whisper. "Does she know?"

And before the doctors can answer, Jed does. "She's known deep down for some time now, sweetheart."

I wipe my face and steady myself. "Yeah, I guess she has."

"Go on in to see her for a few minutes," Dr. Collins says.

Dr. Mark pats my shoulder. "Both of us will be here in the morning when she goes home."

Their white coats are a blur as they walk away, leaving Jed and me alone. I push open the door to Mom's room and hear her rattling breaths.

Her face shines in the glow of the television. She breathes in deep, making the sheets swell before they flutter and settle against her frail body. A tremor in her leg twitches the light cotton. When she groans, I think of Toughie and gently touch her forehead. She stirs when I stroke her hair.

"Hi," she says, blinking.

I swallow and lick my lips. "Hi."

Jed stands on the opposite side of the bed. "We have a few minutes before they kick us out."

Mom reaches toward each of us and we help her sit upright. "What time is it?"

"It's after eight," I say, climbing onto the bed. I spy a large recliner in the corner of the room. "I'm going to stay with you tonight."

A grin spreads across Jed's face, but it vanishes when he looks at Mom. She's shaking her head.

"No, Lily. I want you to ... go home." She slides back into a lying position and grimaces. She reaches for my face and cups my chin. "You need rest, too."

My chin tightens and quivers in her hand. "But, Mom ... " I stop myself. I want to tell her that I have my whole life to rest. But I don't say it. I hold it in because I don't want her to worry about me. I twist the corner of the sheet and look into her tired hazel eyes. "I want to be with you every second I can because I love you," I whisper. I scoot alongside her.

She wraps her arms around me. "I love you, too."

I linger in her powdery scent while she rocks me gently. "I'm sorry," she whispers. The warmth of her breath in my hair and the knowing in her words sends shivers through me.

Jed comes around to my side of the bed. "Your mom will be out of here in twelve hours. Let's let her sleep."

I feel crushed, but I take a deep breath and try to put on a happy face. "Twelve hours, Mom." I tuck the sheets around her and lean over her. "We'll be back for you in the morning."

"Bring me good coffee," she says with a wink.

"And a muffin," I add.

Jed waves and I blow her a kiss just before the door swings closed. We ride the elevator in silence before walking through the parking lot. I rest my temple against the truck window and feel the rumble of the engine. Drizzle swirls around the headlights. The truck bounces over speed bumps, making the side of my head bang against the window.

The smooth asphalt on the empty street glistens. "Days!" I shout, banging my head on purpose this time. "Days!"

Jed's knuckles whiten. He shakes his head and says, "We just have to take it one day at a time."

"That's what Mom told me years ago when Dad was in the hospital. We've been living that way ever since."

Jed steers with his knee as he cracks his knuckles. "I'm sorry."

I can't help my sarcastic tone. "It's not your fault." I rub my neck. "Mom said we needed to be strong and we've been that. We've been so damn strong. And now, she's been suffering because"—I wipe my nose on the back of my wrist—"because of me. If I'd been a little stronger, none of this would be happening." I grip my knees. "Just one more sting. That's all she wanted. One."

"She was wrong to ask you to do that," Jed says as we pull into my driveway.

His words stun me. "Wrong?"

"Yes. Without all the paperwork in place, it was wrong." He looks intently at me when he says this. "You did the right thing by staying strong."

My hands tremble as a sense of relief comes over me. "I don't want to be strong," I whisper just as Pepper starts barking with excitement.

The house is dark except for an occasional flicker from the TV. It casts a blue hue through the living room windows. I long to see the golden glow of the porch light. I step out of the truck, prepared to feel my way through the darkness and up the stairs.

Jed hooks my arm in his and leads me toward the house. We're being careful to step around the lily garden when the porch light comes on. Light washes over the flowers and I stop.

"Each lily blossom lasts for one day before it dies off. When it does, the next bud will open and have its day," I murmur.

"One day at a time," Jed says, nodding.

I tilt my head and squint at him. "Exactly." I point at the White Lace. "This is the same blossom that was open earlier today," I say and bend closer to the flower. "It should be wilted by now, but it's still hanging on."

I sense Jed leaning in to admire it. Together, we take in its beauty.

"I don't want her to suffer for my sake anymore, Jed."

Shauna opens the screen door and lets Pepper out to charge us. Pepper zigzags around us, pounces on a rock, and bolts back into the house with it.

Trent pops his head around Shauna. "You coming in?"

"No shit, Sherlock." Shauna holds the door open for us. She's wearing a pair of my sweats and the house looks tidier than when we left. "I hope you don't mind," she says, tugging at the pants.

I spot Mom's files stacked up on the counter and notice that the dishes have been put away. "No, I don't mind at all. Thanks." I wonder if they looked at the files and make a mental note to ask Shauna later, when we're alone.

"How is she?" Trent asks, straddling a kitchen chair. He tightens his face as though he's bracing for the answer.

I can't bring myself to reply and am thankful when Jed does. "She's resting," he says.

I go to the cupboard for the can of coffee and spot boxes of brownie, cake, and muffin mix. I set all the boxes and the coffee next to the pot.

"No coffee for me," Jed says. "It's too late for caffeine."

"It's for Mom. She asked for coffee in the morning."

Jed blushes and rubs his whiskered jaw. "Right. And a muffin."

I slide the boxes to the center of the counter. "Mom's birthday is in a couple of days. If I throw her a surprise party tomorrow, will you all come?"

"I think that's a wonderful idea, Lily." Jed stands and pats my shoulder. "Of course we'll be here."

"I'll bring frozen grapes and chips and salsa," Trent says. "My specialties." He rubs his knuckles on his chest and blows on them.

"Sounds good." Pepper shoves her rock into my thigh, egging me on to play with her. "And Pepper will bring the rocks."

Shauna starts reading the instructions on the box of brownies. "I'll make these. I'd be happy to."

"Thank you," I say, holding my hand over my heart. I look into each of my friends' faces before resting my eyes on the stack of files behind them.

"I'll be back in the morning," Trent says. "I'll have my mom call me in sick for school."

"Me too," Jed says, then laughs. "I mean, I'll call in sick, too."

"Please invite your mom and dad," I say to Shauna. "You too, Trent. Let's say noon so they can come on their lunch hour."

"Noon?" Jed raises and eyebrow. "How can we pull off a surprise if your Mom is already home?"

"Trust me," I say, because I know that once Mom comes home, she'll spend most of her time in her bedroom. "It'll be fine."

Jed makes a round of good-byes and tells me he'll be here at eight sharp. When he's gone, I find the courage to fill Trent and Shauna in.

"She won't allow treatment?" Shauna gasps.

Trent stands in the doorway and runs his fingers through his hair. "Has my dad done everything he can to help her?" His neck turns bright red.

"Yes, Trent, he's done everything that Mom will allow." I hug him and see him out to the porch. "And turning her care over to Dr. Mark says a lot."

"I see," Trent says. "I wish there was something I could do." He shoves his hands in his pockets and walks to his truck. I see his silhouette swing a leg and kick the door.

He flashes his high beams at me and I wave. "Being here is something," I call. "See you tomorrow."

I dim the lights in the kitchen, blow my nose into a napkin, and toss the wad into the trash. A shimmer of blue satin stripes catches my attention. Jed's clip-on tie from this morning. I pluck it from the garbage, wipe it off and lay it gently on the counter. "It has one more purpose to serve," I whisper, lifting the files into my arms.

Sixteen

The TV casts a warm glow in the living room where Shauna's hugging Pepper on the sofa. Both of them squint when I touch the lamp and brighten the room. I set the files on the table. "Did you and Trent open these?"

Shauna lifts her head from Pepper. "No. I was tempted, but I ... we didn't."

She comes to my side when I open the first file, labeled *Lily*. It's thin compared to the others. Underneath the will there's documents and legal forms giving Jed guardianship of me. Mom's signature is scratched onto each one.

"These expire when you turn eighteen," Shauna says, pointing to a clause. "Less than two years."

I bind the file and snap the rubber band. "I know," I say, switching my file for the one marked *House*. The deed to our property is on top. The mortgage statement is stapled to it and shows a zero balance.

"Your house is totally paid for," Shauna says. She looks out the window toward the pasture. "That's good."

I turn my gaze toward the photograph above the TV. Dad seems to look back at me. "Mom paid off the house with Dad's life insurance. She said it was what he would've wanted."

The rest of the papers in the house file are utility bills and warranties for every single appliance. I chuckle as I flip through them. "She's so organized."

The medical file is the thickest of the three. The first document assigns Jed as her medical power of attorney. I wince as I turn the page, revealing her living will.

Shauna covers the page with her palm. "Maybe it's not a good idea to look at these."

I push her hand away, flip the page, and catch my breath.

Shauna gasps. "Stop, Lily. You don't need this right now."

But I do. More than anything, right at this very moment, I need to understand Mom. Of all the words on the page, only three come into focus—the three she'd also said to me. I whisper them out loud. "*Do not resuscitate.*" Seeing it in black and white makes is all too real. It might as well be a neon sign flashing *DNR*.

I wince, thinking about all the past clients who left our clinic empty handed after signing a DNR for their animal. This is my mother.

The next paper shakes in my hands. It's addressed to Dr. Collins. I clear my throat and read it out loud.

"*This is my formal written request for medication to end my life. I have complied with all the laws of Oregon's Death with Dignity Act and am of sound mind. Two oral requests were made to you, and this written one serves as my third and final request.*

I ask that you respect my decision and grant my wish to go gracefully. There is no quality to my life, only suffering."

I run my finger across Mom's signature. "Oh, Mom." I slowly turn to the next page. Shauna and I scan it together. It says the same thing, except it's a legal form from the state.

Shauna's face pales when we get to the bottom. Jed Abrams' signature fills one witness line. The name in the second line reads *Marjorie Lauri*.

My eyes snap back and forth, from Shauna to the signature. "Did you know? Did your mom tell you? Is that why you've been coming around more?" My heart skips with every question.

Shauna stares at the paper. She lingers on it for what seems like forever until I push her arm. "I need to know the truth," I say. I lower my voice and search her eyes. "Did your mom put you up to coming here?"

Puddles in Shauna's eyes release a stream when she blinks. "I had no idea, Lily. My mom doesn't talk about her lawyer stuff to me. I swear."

"Okay," I say under my breath. I'm so relieved to know she's here on her own, and I feel bad for having the fleeting thought that her being here wasn't genuine. "I'm sorry." I rub my face before flipping through the rest of the papers.

They're all medical records in dated order, starting with when Mom was first diagnosed and running through four years ago, when she switched to the alternative medicines. CAT scans. Lesions. Spinal tap. Brain stem. Pain. The phrases are repeated over and over until bee venom therapy appears.

I'm surprised to see that a small batch of records from Dr. Collins office follow. The first is dated two months ago. "She went back to him," I say, trying to understand.

The last record has a note from Dr. Collins. I wipe my eyes and show the paper to Shauna. "I can't make this out."

She holds the page in front of her and reads it to me.

"*Sophia's disease has progressed rapidly. She continues to refuse traditional treatment and rejects the idea of nursing home care. She is aware her time is limited even with medical aid. She is terminal. Second oral request for Death with Dignity noted."*

I crumple next to Pepper. "Am I a bad, selfish person for not wanting her to go?" I sob into Pepper's neck.

Shauna sits on the floor in front of me and swipes my hair out of my eyes. "Of course not. She's your mom and you want her to live forever."

Pepper licks my face and pulls herself out from under me. I roll onto my back. "Even when she's suffering?"

Shauna rolls onto her side, facing me, and tucks a throw pillow under her head. "Get some sleep, Lily."

A million thoughts race through my exhausted brain as I stare at the ceiling. A mundane thought creeps in. *I should paint the ceiling.* I focus on two greasy stains in the jagged plaster. Stains Mom and I made when we balled up the creamy centers of Oreo cookies, threw them up to make them stick, and waited for them to drop. Mom's ball dropped first so she got to eat mine, too. I shake my head and smile, remembering the silly game. *I'll never paint that ceiling. Ever.*

Then I recall how Mom used a whole row of cookies to make me the biggest ball of cream center ever, and I realize I'll never forget those small moments. The memories and love will live on even after the stains are gone. A hundred coats of paint can't take that away from me. Nothing can. Nothing.

Seventeen

The scent of chocolate fills my nose before my eyes are even open. I wipe slobber off my cheek and find Pepper standing an inch away, breathing onto my face. I scoop up her chin and kiss her between the eyes. "What smells so good?" I peel myself off of the couch.

Shauna pops her head out of the kitchen. "I'm baking. The muffins are cooling and the brownies are almost done." She flashes a wide smile.

I smile back and giggle. She's got a smear of brownie mix on her forehead and has no clue. She's wearing one of my shirts and my favorite pair of jeans. I can't complain.

"You look fresh this morning," I say, hobbling over to her. "I'm stiff." I swipe the chocolate from her face and lick my finger. "It's a good look for you."

I check the clock while Shauna runs to the bathroom. Six forty-five. "What the heck time did you get up?" I call to her.

She returns spit-shined a few minutes later and pours us some coffee. "Pepper woke me up about five. I've let her out and fed her already." She dumps blueberry muffins onto a dishtowel. "I hope you don't mind that I made these, too. I figured, as long as I was up." She makes a fist and playfully shakes it at Pepper.

"I appreciate it, Shauna. Thanks." I test my coffee, wrapping my hands around the cup, warming my fingers. "After I shower, I'll run to the basement for birthday plates and balloons." I head up the stairs as I finish my thought. "I have to be out of here before eight o'clock, though. Mom's expecting us first thing."

"I'll decorate while you're gone," Shauna calls to me.

I strip out of my slept-in clothes and rummage through my closet to find something partylike but not fancy. Definitely not fancy. Mom would know something was up if I showed up in a skirt. I settle for khaki capris and a brown sleeveless T-shirt with a tiger lily on it. *Mom will like this.*

I'm in and out of the shower in five minutes flat. I spit on a tissue and cover two bloody razor marks.

Good thing the capris are long enough to hide shaving wounds.

From the top of the stairs, I spot Shauna. She's on the landing, taping a pink balloon to the railing. She glances up at me. Her black eyes shine. "I found balloons!"

My heart sinks as I descend the stairs. *I wanted to do it.* I shut down my impulse to whine and compliment her instead. "You're the best, Shauna." I really mean it. It feels good to have her here.

It doesn't take long for the two of us to scatter the balloons throughout the kitchen and living room. We wind crepe paper through the banister and hang curly streamers in the doorway.

"I'll bring her in through the back door and take her straight to her room." I scan the rooms. "She'll be surprised."

A look of worry spreads over Shauna's face. "Will she really stay in her room? Won't she need to come out to use the bathroom?"

"She'll stay in her room." I slide into a kitchen chair. "Her kidneys are damaged from her disease. She can't go on her own anymore."

Shauna just raises her eyebrows.

"I should've known," I say, watching the second hand on the clock.

"How could you know?" She lays a hand over mine and pats it. "Don't do that to yourself."

"I've been her caretaker for four years!" I stand up when I hear the honk of Jed's truck. "She was hardly ever using the bathroom." I squeeze my eyes shut. "I know that's a bad sign for sick animals. I should've been aware of that for my own mother, right?"

Shauna grabs my face and forces me to look at her. "It is not your fault. It's nobody's fault."

I hug her. "Thanks for being here for me."

Jed honks again.

Shauna and Jed exchange hellos before Jed and I drive off. He smiles at the rearview mirror. "That girl sure has come around."

"Yes, she has." I chuckle. "All on her own, too."

Jed looks at me like I'm not speaking English.

"She's a good friend," I say.

Jed shoots me an exaggerated happy face and opens his eyes wide.

Together we chime, "Friends are good," and laugh.

I get quiet, trying to find the courage to tell Jed what I've seen. I have to come clean. Finally, as we pull under the valet canopy, I blurt it out. "Don't tell Mom, but I looked through all the files last night."

He doesn't seem shocked until it sinks in. As he turns off the engine, his face grays. I know he's thinking about Mom's wishes. About the papers he signed as a witness for her request for Death with Dignity.

"I'm not mad at you," I say. I lay my hand on his arm. "For the past year, every time something came on

197

the news about mercy killing, assisted suicide, or Death with Dignity, she'd listen closely. Riveted. The idea's been in her head for a long time. I wasn't willing to trade her agony for mine before, but I'm done putting myself first."

The valet interrupts us, taking Jed's keys and leaving us on the curb. We stand side by side, looking up at the hospital windows. "She doesn't want you to be in agony," Jed says. "I'm sure she didn't tell you about the papers because she's protecting you. And because she's probably afraid you won't approve."

He's so right. That's all she needs, my disapproval. I press my fingers to my chest and swallow. I can only nod as we make our way to the entrance. A swoosh of air sucks us in as the double doors magically open. The scent of ammonia burns my throat.

Jed blows his nose. "It was Mrs. A's," he says when he notices me looking at his purple-flowered hanky. He stuffs it into his pocket.

Our reflections stretch before us once again. Elevator music pipes in as we rise.

A nurse rides with us and I scoot closer to Jed. "I just want to know," I say. "Did you get Shauna's mom to sign, too?"

The nurse squeezes by us when the doors open. Jed holds onto my elbow and leads me off and into the hallway. He checks the room numbers and starts walking. "Marjorie Lauri is an old friend of your par..."

He clears his throat. "Of your mom's. Plus, she's a fine attorney. Helped me out of many jams in my time. I did suggest her to your mom, yes."

"Okay," I say, but I can't help wondering who else knows. I hear Miss Andre's voice in my head: *I've read your case file.*

What does it really matter who else knows? Who cares. It's none of their business.

Dr. Collins and Dr. Mark are leaning against the nurse's station as we approach. They barely get out "Hello" when I lay into them.

"You must honor my Mom's wishes," I begin.

Dr. Mark's eyes widen. Dr. Collins stiffens. Jed fidgets with his fingers and then cracks them.

I stare at the checkered floor and keep talking. "I've read through her files and I know she's done everything she's supposed to do to make this happen, with your help. If you don't help her, she'll do it anyway. I know it. She has everything she needs at our clinic." I look Dr. Collins in the eye and step toward him. "Do no harm, remember? Isn't ignoring her wishes doing harm?" I look at Dr. Mark. "Is it legal for you to *refuse* a request to die?"

Jed looks around before meeting my glance. The corner of his mouth curls as he nods at me.

"You know I put that calf down," I say to Dr. Collins, just loud enough for him to hear. "It was hard, but it was the right thing to do." I choke back tears as I stand tall and look from Dr. Mark to Dr. Collins. "Now you doctors need to do right by Mom. You know it's what she wants."

Dr. Collins holds up a palm. "It's already in motion, Lily."

"Her request was approved," Dr. Mark says.

His words slap me off of my high horse. I slump and stumble back. No arguing? No offer of hope? Nothing? Don't they know I would bargain my life for hers? For a cure. For anything to make this all go away. But as they stand there in their stark whites, I realize they are angels, not God. Mom will get her wish.

I press my lips together and force a smile. "Thank you," I whisper.

"The medication will be going home with her today," Dr. Mark says. "I've spoken to her about it and have offered to be there when ... she's ready. She's a brave woman." Muscles in his jaw pop. He looks at me intently. "*You* are a brave young lady," he adds.

Jed holds up the brown lunch bag that holds Mom's coffee and muffin. "We'd better go in before this gets cold."

Brave. I suddenly don't feel that way. I'm the first to go in. I tiptoe around the curtain, shocked at what I find.

Mom's fully clothed and sitting up watching a game show, rooting the contestants on. "Big money, big money," she yells, laughing. She waves us in and holds her arms out to me.

"Hi, Mom. Your eye looks better," I say, hugging her side.

Jed sets the bag on the tray table. "Your order, Madame."

Dr. Collins and Dr. Mark stand there like twin plaster statues.

Mom wiggles a finger at them. "Ah, it's good cop ... bad cop." She chuckles into her coffee.

Dr. Mark laughs. "Does that mean you feel like a prisoner here, Sophia? That breaks my heart."

"I think it means we take on a good-guy, bad-guy, role," Dr. Collins says, sucking the humor out of the room. He blushes a little and gets flustered. "Bad cop has got to go on rounds," he pronounces and cracks the door. When we all laugh at that, his face relaxes.

"There're no bad cops here," I say. I tilt my head and blink at him as he ducks into the hall.

He points to his watch and mouths, "I'll see you later."

I realize Trent's invited him to the party. I mouth, "Okay."

Mom's too into her game show to catch on. "Ask for a vowel, stupido!"

"Sophia," Dr. Mark says, turning down the TV. "Gretchen will be in with your papers, and then you're free to go."

My gut lurches. *Free to go.*

Mom doesn't miss a beat. "I made bail!" She laughs. The forced bed rest seems to have made her more alert. I've seen this before. It's short term, but it sure is nice to see her joking around again.

Jed laughs, too.

I join in, with a fake laugh designed to throw her off of the fact that I know the exact price of her bail. A vial of deadly medicine. A liquid barbiturate. A lethal drink. One that will stop her from being a prisoner in her own body. I play along because she has no clue that I know.

As if she's reading my thoughts, Mom asks, "What is it, tiger? Why the long face?"

I look to Jed and Dr. Mark. "Nothing, Mom."

"It's this place," she says just as Gretchen walks in. "No offense, Gretchen."

Gretchen glues a hand to her hip, pretending to be insulted. She holds a white paper bag in the other hand. "Got your papers and your medication. Just sign here."

Mom signs without hesitation, takes the bag, and reaches for Jed to help her stand. "You take care... Gretchen. Be easy on your joints. Try the herbs... we talked about."

I flash a smile at Gretchen. Mom must really like her to have said all that.

"I will," Gretchen says. "A new game plan for my arthritis is a good idea."

They exchange a quick hug before Jed helps Mom into a wheelchair. "This electric chair is spiffy," Mom says, powering forward. "Let's go ..." Her voice trails off as she leaves Jed and me in the dust.

Jed chases after her. "Sophia!"

Gretchen's stripping the bed when I peek back into the room. "I'm throwing a little party for Mom today. Her birthday is a few days away, so I thought I'd surprise her."

"That's nice," Gretchen says, squeezing the pillow out of its case. "Oh, am I invited? Are you inviting me?"

"Yes. If you can come, that'd be nice." I poke my head into the hall. Jed and Mom are almost at the exit sign. "I know we're practically strangers, but Mom would like it. So would I."

"I'd like that too, Lily."

"Maybe you can ride with Dr. Collins? It starts at noon."

Gretchen makes a sour face and then laughs. "I'll take my lunch break then."

"We're having brownies and coffee," I say and bolt out to find Mom and Jed. They're by the elevator, whirling in a slow circle. "Having fun?" I tease.

"To the homestead, Jed," Mom orders, and points. Her arm locks and spasms. She forces it down with her other arm and presses it to her lap. She winces and smiles simultaneously.

That's when I realize this burst of energy is all a façade. She's the one being brave now and acting like all is dandy.

I continue to play along, for her sake and mine. It's like we both know what the real deal is, but it's easier to put on a brave front and try to cope. She's leaving here and will never return. We're taking her home and it's only a matter of time before ... I swallow a bitter film at the back of throat, wink at her, and press the elevator button.

"To the homestead, Jed," I say.

Eighteen

I scrunch into the back seat while Mom and Jed bicker about the price of gas. Part of me is glad to hear their small talk. Another part of me—the one that's lodged in my throat—wants to shout, *Who cares what the price of gas will be next summer!* I can't let myself envision next summer. I can only think about today. *One day at a time.*

When we roll into the driveway, I check the clock on the dashboard. Its green glow illuminates nine forty-five. Two hours till party time.

Jed lifts the wheelchair out of the back of the truck. I crawl out and open Mom's side. The peach on her cheeks has faded. She looks tired. A few hours of up-and-about time takes its toll on her. I know the routine.

She's learned not to fight the fatigue and has to nap every few hours.

"Let's get you in to rest," I say. She swings her legs toward me. I grab hold of her calves to help her swivel. I suck in a breath, feeling how swollen she is. "Oh, Mom." I skim my hands along her legs, down to her ankles. They are the same size as her calves.

She shoos my hands away. "I need to elevate them."

But I know better now. The build-up of fluid in her body dimples her skin.

Jed pulls the wheelchair around and sets the brakes. He gently nudges me and, in one swift move, he scoops Mom out of the truck and places her in the chair.

"It'll be easiest to go in the back door," I say, cutting in front of them. "No stairs."

Jed stops on the brick walkway and looks to the shredded bark path that winds around to the back. "As you wish." He pops the chair into a wheelie and pushes ahead.

Mom tilts her head back and smiles up at him. "Nose hair," is all I hear her say after I swing the back door open wide.

The wheelchair doesn't seem like it will quite fit through the door frame. It doesn't help that Pepper keeps trying to make her way to Mom. She's ballistic. Nudging, pushing, pawing to get at Mom. I block her.

"Go!" I shout and point. Her ears go limp as she follows my command. She sulks away, disappearing around the corner. She returns not a minute later. This time, her zebra is stuffed in her mouth. She shakes with anticipation.

I pull as Jed pushes. He counts to three and with all my might, I yank Mom into the house. I fall on my butt. Pepper seizes the opportunity and leaps over my legs. She shoves the zebra onto Mom's lap and plants kisses wherever her tongue lands. Mom soothes her by holding her face. "Settle. Settle."

Pepper bolts away with her toy.

Mom studies the chipped door frame and shakes her head. "Three Stooges."

Jed and I look at each other and start laughing. "Next time we'll fold the chair and carry you in," Jed says.

"Let's get you to your room," I say, wheeling her down the hall. I tuck her in after Jed lifts her into bed.

"You want something to eat or drink?" Jed asks, handing her the remote.

Mom yawns and smacks her lips. "Iced tea, please."

I glance at her alarm clock. "You nap for a while. I'll wake you up at lunchtime." I hear Jed mumbling in the kitchen and I force a cough.

When Jed returns with the tea, Mom asks him, "Who were you talking to?"

I see his Adam's apple bobble in his neck. "Pepper," he says.

Mom wrinkles her eyebrows. She points to the floor next to her bed. "She's right there."

I stifle a laugh and cover his butt. "It's okay, Jed. Everyone talks to themselves once in a while." I snap my fingers for Pepper to come. "Get some rest, Mom," I whisper as we leave her alone.

Shauna's arranging cheese and sausage on a plate when I come into the kitchen. "Oh, good idea." A new pot of coffee burps on the counter. "Candles!" I say. "We need candles."

"I'll pick some up on my way back," Jed offers. He turns his wrist and winds his watch. "Toughie's body is getting picked up in fifteen minutes. I have to go."

Shauna and I walk him out to the porch. Pepper leaps over the lily garden and I hold my breath until she lands on the other side. She just missed the White Lace. *Mom has to see it.*

Just as Jed pulls out, Trent pulls in and parks right in front of the door. "Help me with these," he says, holding a tray out the window. "Put this in the freezer."

The truck engine hums as I peek under the foil. "Yum!" Frozen red grapes are piled in the center of a ring of chocolate-covered strawberries. Shauna takes the other tray and Trent drives away. He parks down the hill, behind the barn. Twilight whinnies from his stall.

"Take this," I say to Shauna. I prop the door open with my knee and give her the tray.

"Where you going?" She smirks and lifts her chin.

I roll my eyes. "To let Twilight out."

I find Trent stroking Twilight's face and talking softly to him. "Here's your mom," he says to my horse when he sees me. Twilight snorts and stomps.

"He smells Rocky on you," I say, entering the stall.

Trent pushes his hat back. His green eyes melt into the field behind him. "I wanted to ride him over today, but with the trays ... " He pauses and takes my hand. "How's your mom?"

I don't answer. I can't. I give Twi a loving slap on the butt. "Head out!" He trots into the field, then stops and stretches his neck around to look at me. "Not now, sweetlips. I can't ride now." He raises his head and gallops away.

Trent stretches his arm over his head and yelps. "Damn spider!" In a flash, he swings his hat through Ms. Spidey's web, destroying it. He dances around.

"What did you do that for?" I shout. "You had no right to do that!" I search the ground for Ms. Spidey. She's nowhere to be found. I cover my face.

Trent's arms fold around me. "It's just a spider. I'm sorry." He peers into my eyes.

"Don't look at me like I'm crazy," I say, pushing away. "I liked that spider." I shrug, knowing he can't understand. Ms. Spidey wasn't harming anyone. She was my little guard of the stable, keeping the mosquitoes at bay. She was something I looked forward to.

Something I could count on. "I'm sorry," I say. "I'm glad you're here and didn't mean to yell at you."

"I know." He brushes the back of his fingers against my cheek. He leans in closer as Jed's truck pulls in. I step away and wave Jed down to the barn. He sticks the truck in park and shuts off the engine just as a little pink head pops up in the passenger seat.

"Pisser!" I squeal. Then another pink snout appears. "Sunbeam!"

"Your mom ever get live bacon for a present?" Jed palms little Sunbeam and hands her to me. He winks. "Let's let Trent here hold Pisser, shall we?"

Trent holds the piglet away from him. "Pisser? Did you say Pisser?" His eyebrows pull together and I crack up.

Jed hauls a crate out of his truck and balances it on his shoulder. When we get to the front yard, Pepper gets a whiff of the pigs and comes running. Pisser and Sunbeam seem relieved when we put them in the crate and lock the door. Pepper circles the cage, whining to get at them. The pigs move from corner to corner, squealing with worry.

We've all been busy doing something—sweeping, arranging food, straightening up—when Shauna says, "People should be arriving any minute now."

I finish setting out iced tea and coffee and hurry to get the fruit out of the freezer. "Thanks for your help, everyone."

Shauna makes room on the table for the cheese platter.

Jed steals a slice of sausage and talks with his mouth full. "Got the candles," he murmurs, pulling a box from his shirt pocket.

I set the sheet of brownies in the center of the table and create a five and a zero using the candles. "The table looks beautiful. Simple, but beautiful."

A slight knock on the door makes us all turn at once. Dr. Mark, Dr. Collins, and Gretchen are smiling at us through the screen.

"Mom's in her room," I whisper. "Come on in." I poke my head out to check on Pepper. She's lying on her side with her back against the crate. The piglets nuzzle tufts of her hair, snuffling at every inch of her coat. She lies frozen to the spot, bug-eyed. No amount of company is going to pull her attention away. Even a truck full of rocks couldn't persuade her to come in.

"I think Pepper's in love," I say to Jed.

He glances behind me and chuckles. "Or hungry."

I smack his arm. "Jed!"

Shauna's mom arrives within minutes of Trent's mom. They're polar opposites. Marjorie, dressed in a business suit, turns off her pager; Mrs. Collins, in her usual tailored jogging suit, hands out napkins. By the time everyone has something to drink, the mood in the room feels somber.

"Okay, everyone," I say. "This is a party. I'm happy you all are here, and Mom will be too. But you have to wipe those grim looks off your faces before I bring her out here. Got it?"

"Got it," they all answer, and perk up.

A voice pipes in from the porch. "Got it."

I shoot a look at Shauna, who shrugs and says, "Don't look at me."

I grab the handle of the door and lock it as I glare through the screen.

Betsy squints, and Emily crosses her arms over her chest and slouches.

Nineteen

hat are you two doing here?" I snap.

Emily pops her gum and motions to Betsy. "We came to apologize." Her minty breath floats between us.

Shauna appears at my side with her fist on her hip. "Why aren't you in school?"

Betsy licks her wounded lip. "We got suspended, too," she says, elbowing Emily. "We're sorry."

Emily's eyes flutter before they land on me. "I'm sorry, too." She teeters on her tiptoes and looks into the kitchen before looking back at me. "For everything," she whispers. She glances around me again and calls, "Hi, Trent, Dr. and Mrs. Collins."

"Trent," I say. It all makes sense now. I turn to make eye contact with Trent and he quickly pretends to be busy picking at the bottom of his shoe. I see Dr. Mark check his watch. I unlock the door and step aside. "Oh, just come on in," I say. "We're throwing my mom a surprise party. I have to get her now." I stress the last word as they sidestep around me. "Don't you start any crap," I say as they pass.

Trent finally looks up. He smiles and nods at me. Shauna covers her mouth and bends forward, holding her side.

I lead Jed into Mom's room. She stirs and blinks.

"Mom," I whisper. "Someone's here to see you." I pull back her blankets and rub her arm.

"What? Who?" She pulls herself up. "Bring them in here."

Jed scoops her out of bed and sets her into the chair before she can object. "You first, Lily."

"What's going on?" Mom scrunches her hair and then smoothes it. "Who's here?" she demands as we roll her toward the kitchen.

As soon as we appear in the doorway, everyone shouts, "Surprise!"

She shakes her head, looking totally confused.

I clap and hug her around her neck. "Happy birthday, Mom!"

She sits back, taking everyone in one at a time. "Gretchen." She reaches out as Gretchen goes to her and lays a set of white towels on Mom's lap. "I shopped all day for these," she says, pointing to the hospital name printed on the hems.

Mom laughs and takes Gretchen's hands. They swing their hands together and smile.

Dr. Mark and Dr. Collins greet her next. "No white coats?" Mom teases.

The doctors each set a bunch of flowers on top of the towels. "Happy birthday, Sophia," Dr. Mark says.

Dr. Collins shocks us all when he bends and hugs Mom. She hugs him back. "You're a good cop, too," she says, smiling.

He straightens his tie and clears his throat. "Thank you," he says, before hurrying over to his wife.

Mom nods to Shauna and Trent. She looks quizzically at Emily, but then smiles. "It's been a long time."

"This is Betsy," Emily says. The girls sway in their spots. "Happy birthday," they say in unison.

Jed claps and wipes the awkward moment out of the air. "One more gift!" He turns Mom in her chair and rolls her backward to the screen door.

We crowd around on the porch. Emily and Betsy race to the porch swing. The chains creak as they sit. "I always loved this swing," Emily says. She looks up and smiles when she catches me watching them.

Jed covers Mom's eyes and turns her to face the yard. The crate sits at the bottom of the stairs. Pepper is still glued to it and the piglets are sleeping soundly.

Jed counts to three and uncovers Mom's eyes. She looks at the crate and back to Jed. She looks down the driveway and back to Jed.

I call for Pepper. When she comes to my side I say, "There, her furry butt is out of the way now."

Mom rubs her chin and grins. "Pigs, Jed?" She leans closer when the pigs wake up and bound around the crate. "Very original." She grapples for my hand. "Help me up."

"I'll get her," Jed says. He points to Trent and me. "You two get the bacon."

Trent hops off the porch. "I call the one that doesn't piss."

I laugh at the reactions on the faces of our guests. "Here ya go." I hand Trent a piglet and take the other one in my arms. Pepper's rearing up, sniffing away, as I take it to Mom.

She sits on the porch step, nose to nose with it. "Very cute, Jed." Pepper scoots as close to Mom as possible and gently licks the piglet.

Everyone smiles and says, "Aw."

"They've just been weaned from Mama Sow," Jed says, all proud. "A bucket of mush will have them plump just in time for Christmas."

I nudge Jed and shake my head. "Christmas?" I mouth to him.

"For ham," he says, like he doesn't get my drift.

At that, the piglet Trent holds squeals and pees on his boot. "Dang it!" He shoves Pisser at me. "I said I wanted the one that *didn't* piss."

"That's not really possible now, is it?" I bite my lower lip to keep from giggling and squint at him. "Besides, you deserve it." I cock my head in Emily's direction.

Trent blushes and shrugs. "Touché."

"So this is Sunbeam," Mom says, stroking its plump belly.

"Mom," I say, handing Pisser to Shauna, "I have a gift for you too. Besides the party, I mean. It's something I know you'll love."

She passes Sunbeam to Jed and stands slowly when I take her hand. We walk a few steps to the garden. Her breaths come out in quick pants. I point to the White Lace lily.

"Amazing." Her eyes glisten, reflecting hundreds of orange, yellow, and pink lilies. The hardy stalk of the White Lace is full of buds. One blossom is fully open. It shimmers and glows in front of the others.

Mom spreads her palm open. "It's bigger than my hand." She leans into me. "I do love it."

"Happy birthday, Mom," I say, hugging her gently and kissing her cheek.

I guide her back to the porch. Jed scoops her up and she balks. "Set me down."

"Let's eat!" I call out. Emily and Betsy look up from where they've gotten comfy on the lawn. The piglets scurry around them as Pepper watches. "Coming?" I ask.

I instruct anyone who's touched livestock to wash up before they make a plate. Trent comes up behind me and pokes me in the ribs. I jump and turn to face him.

"Payback." He smirks. "For giving me Pisser."

I pull him aside. "Serves you right. You're the little shit who put Emily and Betsy up to coming here, aren't you?" I squint at him. "Why would you do that?"

He shakes his head. "I only told them to grow up and stop messing with you. That if they didn't, I wouldn't talk to either of them again." He stares at his boots.

I touch his chin until he looks at me. "Thank you," I say. "I know you're trying to look out for me, but if they're only here because of your threat, I don't need them."

I catch Emily watching us. She shrugs and blinks before asking Shauna to pass the tea. I stand aside and watch everyone mingle. Mom's at the head of the table, smiling and laughing. I close my eyes for a moment and listen, soaking in her laughter. When she clears her throat and says, "I'd like to make a toast," my eyes spring open.

She holds up a glass. There's a long pause while she brings it down and clears her throat again. "It means a lot to have this last party…"

A collective sense of shock fills the room. Marjorie holds her napkin to her eye. Shauna and Trent just stare at me. Everyone else stops what they're doing.

Jed touches her shoulder and interrupts, "Sophia, let's not…"

"No, Jed, let her speak. She deserves to finish," I say. I wink at her.

She winks back. Her eyes become watery when she reaches for my hand. "I'm grateful that Lily invited each of you." She takes a sip of tea while we wait. "Thank you for being here for me… and for Lily."

My heart skips a beat. They're here for me, too. I feel a little ashamed that I'm just realizing this now. I take a deep breath and raise my glass. "It means a lot to me, too."

"We're here for both of you," Jed says. He raises his glass. "That'll never change."

Everyone lifts their drinks and begins clinking glasses. "Happy birthday."

Mom pats my hand. "Friends are good."

I raise my glass. "Let's have dessert!" I light the candles and we sing to Mom.

The flicker of the flames illuminates her face as she leans forward. "I wish you all love and happiness," she says, and blows out her candles.

Everyone claps as I pass around plates. We mingle and tell stories for some time before Dr. Collins, Dr. Mark, and Gretchen huddle around me. "Thank you for including us."

"Thank you for staying," I say, knowing it's way past the end of their lunch breaks.

Gretchen pulls me aside while the doctors say their good-byes to Mom. "Lily," she says in a serious tone. "Your Mom suggested I try the bee venom therapy for my arthritis." She shows me her knobby hands. "Would you do that for me?"

I take a deep breath through my nose and exhale. I look at her swollen joints and nod. "I think we could work something out."

"Fair enough," she says. "We'll talk." She gives me a one-armed hug and catches up to her ride.

Emily leaves Betsy by the screen door and glides over to me. "When you didn't call me, I thought stopping by would be a good idea. We didn't mean to barge in, but thanks for letting us stay."

I stack dirty paper cups and turn to her. "I've had a lot to do and calling you was really the last thing on my mind. Nothing personal, even though it should be, after the hallway smack-down." I give her a slight sideways grin.

"Yeah, about that." She looks at the ceiling. "When I found out about you and Trent, I flipped. I wanted to talk to you on the phone and say I'm sorry. Not just because Trent wants me to, but because I am sorry."

I look over at Trent when she says that. He's talking with Shauna and Betsy but looking my way. He smiles. My stomach flutters.

"He's always had a crush on you," Emily says, breaking my gaze with a wave.

"I know," I say, smiling at Trent. I pull the trash liner out of the bin, tie it, and hold it out for her. "Take this on your way out, will ya?"

She laughs nervously. "Oh, you're good. I get it." She takes the bag and heads toward the door. She bumps Betsy with her hip and says bye to Shauna and Trent.

They look at the trash and chuckle.

Mrs. Collins and Marjorie come over after saying good-bye to Mom. "You let me know if you need anything," Mrs. Collins says. Marjorie hugs me. "We'll see you soon, honey."

Trent and Shauna see their moms out, leaving just Jed, Mom, and me.

Mom yawns. "Thank you for the party." She rolls back to the table in her spiffy chair.

"I'm glad you had fun." I get busy covering food and wiping crumbs. Jed uncovers the fruit plate and pops a chocolate-covered strawberry into his mouth.

"How's Toughie?" Mom asks. She scrapes brownie crumbs off the table.

Jed chews while Mom waits. I stop cleaning. "Toughie didn't make it," I say.

Her eyes crease in the corners. "Oh, I'm sorry."

I go to her side and kneel. "I put him down." I swallow hard.

Mom strokes the side of my face. "Honey. You did the right thing."

Jed plucks his hanky from his pocket and blows. "I must be going. Mama Sow and Willow need their slop." He plants a kiss on the top of my head and kisses Mom the same way. "I'm five minutes away. You call me for anything. Righto?"

"Of course," I say, walking him to the porch.

Trent pulls up and throws his truck into park. Shauna jumps out of the passenger seat.

"I was wondering what was taking you two so long," I say.

"We settled the pigs into a stall," Shauna says. "Is that okay?"

"Twilight, too," Trent adds. He looks all proud of himself.

"Perfect," I blurt. "Thanks so much!" I scan the pink-streaked sky. A night hawk calls and circles above us. "I didn't think the party would go this late."

"It was so nice. Everyone had a good time." Shauna kicks dirt off her shoe. "Kind of a surprise party for us too, huh?"

"What?" I tilt my head and look to Trent. Then it dawns on me. "Oh, right, Emily and Betsy! Yes. Major shocker that they stayed."

"I know!" Shauna giggles.

Trent breaks up our chatter. "Can we say 'bye to your mom?" he asks. "We have to get going." He thrusts his thumb toward Shauna. "I'm giving her a lift."

Mom's wrapping brownies when we walk in. "You kids take these." She rises from her chair and stumbles when she takes a step.

I rush toward her. "Mom!"

She leans against me and lowers herself back into the chair. "I got dizzy is all."

But I know better. She's in pain. I can see it in the way she winces when she moves, and hear it in every rattled breath she takes. "Trent and Shauna have to go," I tell her. "They came in to say good night."

"Thank you," Mom says. She nods at Trent. "Come back anytime."

He swings his arms. "I plan on it."

Shauna leans in and hugs Mom. "Happy birthday. I'll see you soon."

"I'd like that." Mom takes a deep breath and coughs. "See you."

"I'll talk to you tomorrow," I say to both of them. "Time to get her back to bed."

Shauna goes outside and starts Trent's truck. He pulls me toward the door and kisses my forehead. "Call me anytime. No matter how late it is, okay?"

I wipe a smudge of brownie from the corner of his mouth. "I will. Promise."

Twenty

As soon as they're gone, I turn to Mom. "Did you have fun?" I walk toward her slowly, waiting for her response.

"I'm pooped. Yes." She rolls into the living room, but I stop her.

"Mom." I sit on the coffee table and get eye-level with her. "I can see you're hurting. Let's get you cleaned up and into bed."

She looks to the ceiling and shakes her head. "No. I can do it." Her eyes well up. "I don't want you to."

"But I will. I want to take care of you." I rub her knee until she looks at me.

"I know, tiger." She presses her hand on mine. "I want to do it ... myself."

"Okay." I march over to the hall closet and grab two towels and a wash bin. "I'm going to help you out of your clothes, but I promise not to watch you wash." I drop the towels in her lap and raise my eyebrows.

She purses her mouth and waggles her head. Then she sighs and laughs. "Bossy little thing."

In her bedroom, Mom washes as I divert my eyes. When she's ready, I help her into pajamas and into bed. I tuck a pillow under her swollen calves and crawl up beside her.

"Thank you," she says, stroking my hair.

Pepper lumbers in and hops onto the bed. She licks Mom's hand, and then my face, before lying down at the end of the bed.

I spot the white paper bag on Mom's night table. The little vial lies on its side next to it.

"I read the files," I blurt. I'm ashamed and can't look at her. "I know I promised that I wouldn't, but I did."

She reaches for her water and takes a sip.

"I know what's in that vial." I sit up and face her. My nose starts to tingle. "Even though I wouldn't help you ... before ... " I wipe my eyes on the sheet. "I need to know when you're ready." I search her eyes for an answer and point to the vial. "I want to be with you when you drink it. I don't want you to be all alone." I lay my head on her chest and burst into tears. I feel her heartbeat quicken. I hear her sniff.

"It's for an … emergency. A last resort." She lifts my face until I look at her. "I will tell you." She takes a deep breath. "I love you so very much, Lily." Her words come out smooth, not staggered at all. I know it takes a lot out of her.

"I love you so much, too." I kiss her hand and rest my head on the pillow next to her. "So much."

We lie quietly. Her shallow breathing becomes steady after a few minutes. I crawl out of bed and snap for Pepper to do the same. She lands on the floor with a thud and stretches. "Get some sleep," I whisper when Mom rolls over.

She hums a response as I close her door.

Pepper and I curl onto the couch. She hogs the cushions and is running through a dream before I even close my eyes.

— • —

A ray of early morning light beams on my face. The couch springs squeak and poke. A faint whine comes from the dining room. I open an eye. Pepper's lying by Mom's door, crying to get in.

"Shhh!" I hush her. She pads over to me with her head down. I try to focus on the clock on the TV. "It's only five o'clock, Pepper." She nudges her nose under my arm and whines.

"You need to go out? Come on. Go potty," I say. I stagger to the door and fling it open. She doesn't budge from beside the couch. "Let's go," I insist.

She slinks past me, stops at the stairs, and whines. I step out ahead of her. "Come on!" I demand. She slowly goes down the stairs and sniffs around the lily patch. "If you're not going to pee, then let's go in." I step onto the grass next to the garden.

All the air rushes out of me. "No!" The White Lace blossom is on the ground, wilted. "No!" I leap onto the porch and rush into the house. "Mom!"

Pepper follows as I bolt through the kitchen and swing into Mom's room. It's dim and quiet. Pepper goes to the bed and starts whining again. I hurry to the window to open the blinds.

I go to Mom and touch her hand. Her fingers are cool. Her breathing is faint. She wiggles her fingers and moans. I grasp her hand and press it against my cheek. I rock and cry and kiss her fingers.

"Tiger." She searches for my face and smiles sweetly. "Mercy, Lily." Her eyes are glossy and look past me.

I sit closer, cuddle her against me, and kiss the top of her head. "It's okay, Mom. I'm here." Tears flow down my face. I lean away and grab the vial from the side table. "A last resort."

The corners of her mouth curl and quiver. "I love you." She rests our hands over my heart. "I'm here," she whispers. "Forever."

I sweep her hair away from her forehead and hand her the vial. "Forever." I shake when she takes it and turns the cap. In an instant, our life together flashes before me. Picnics, sand castles, snowmen, bonfires. I wish I could've stayed ten forever. Dad was here. Mom was healthy then.

She drinks down the medication, lies back on her pillow, and squeezes my hand.

My heart races as I drink in her peaceful face. Minutes pass. Her hand relaxes completely in mine, and then she's gone.

I clutch her hand against my chest and rock. "No more suffering, Mom."

Pepper leans heavily into my leg.

The cardinal's song breaks the morning silence. He's calling for his mate. The room fills with an orange glow as the sun rises over the field. It shines on Mom's face. A single tear has puddled in the corner of her eye. I wipe it away and lean in to kiss her. Her lips glisten with leftover death cocktail. I remove the vial from her grip and look at it.

The cardinal sings again, much louder this time. Closer. A female responds and I begin to cry. The vial falls from my fingers. I turn and kiss her cheek. "I'll miss you." I tuck her in one last time, back out of the room, and slowly shut the door behind me.

I sink down the wall and hug my knees. I wail until my jeans are soaked with tears.

—•—

When everyone is seated, I take my place next to the garden. I scan the faces of our friends, neighbors, and clients, including some with their pets. "Thank you for coming," I begin. "A special thank-you to Jed. He's been my rock since I called him on the morning that Mom found peace."

Jed nods and fidgets with his tie. The blue satin stripes glisten in the sunshine.

"Mom arranged this simple, garden-side memorial service. She wasn't afraid of dying. She was afraid of suffering. She's resting now. She will live on forever in my heart." I place a hand to my chest and raise the other, holding her urn. "Mom wished to be sprinkled in her lily garden, and then top that off with a barbecue."

Some of the guests chuckle at that. "That's Sophia for you," I hear someone say.

Jed, Shauna, and Trent come to my side. "Please gather around the garden," I say. A breeze sweeps through the lilies; they bend and sway before reaching back toward the sun. I tip the urn and sprinkle some of her ashes. "Think of my mom whenever you see a day-lily and remember that every blossom has just one day. Enjoy the beauty of each one."

Jed wraps his arms around me, and I squeeze him hard. He wipes my nose with his hanky. I dab my eyes on his tie. He smiles.

Shauna and Trent usher the guests to the buffet provided by Dr. and Mrs. Collins. Pets and animals roam from table to table in search of scraps. Marjorie loses her pie to Sunbeam and Pisser. Dr. Mark and Gretchen toss apples to Twilight and Willow. Mama Sow grunts on the porch, trapping Emily and Betsy in the swing. Others who've come to pay their respects make plates while their animals wander free.

I have an intense feeling of déjà vu. I scan the field, somehow expecting to see the deer from my Heaven dream. I spot a bright red cardinal perched atop the highest point of our pine tree. He sings over and over, so loud and urgent. A female swoops in and lands beside him. He feeds her a seed before they disappear into the thick branches together.

"Sophia would've loved this," Jed says.

I nod. "They're here, you know," I whisper. Pepper appears at my feet with a rock in her mouth. Her cries are muffled. She plops it into the garden and whines.

I stroke her head. "One day at a time."

It's three hours later when the last guest drives away. Jed and I wave before I head to the barn and he goes into the house.

Pisser and Sunbeam are entwined together, sleeping. Twilight whinnies as I approach his stall. I stop abruptly and smile. Ms. Spidey is furiously spinning a new web in the door frame. The stark white threads are aglow against the purplish black sky. "Welcome home," I say to her.

I slip into Twilight's stall and scratch behind his jaw, just below his ears, where he likes it. "Tomorrow, we'll ride," I tell him, and kiss his nose. "I promise."

He nods and neighs. The pigs let out sleepy squeals.

My heart aches as I head up the dirt road toward the house. A nighthawk screeches above. I look to the sky. "I'll be strong," I whisper. I walk slowly past the lily garden. Then, just as I reach the stairs, the porch light flicks on and illuminates my way home.

The End

Joe Albert

About the Author

Lisa Albert knows firsthand about love, loss, and letting go. While *Mercy Lily* is a work of fiction, there are many moments that reflect her own experiences. A lot of research, blood, sweat, and tears went into writing this, her debut novel.

Lisa's other published works for teens include two biographies, *Stephenie Meyer: Author of the Twilight Saga* and *Lois Lowry: The Giver of Stories and Memories*, along with a career how-to book, *So You Want to Be a Film or TV Actor?*

When not writing, Lisa enjoys working as a school library aide, hanging out with family and friends, puttering in her gardens, and hunting for treasures. Visit her online at www.lisaalbert.com.